# Prince Henry St. Clair
# Earl of Orkney

6/23
£2

Note: this is a work of fiction based loosely on Henry St. Clair, Earl of Orkney, also known as "Prince Henry," and his proclaimed voyage to America almost 100 years before Columbus. It was written in the U.K. with British spellings.

ISBN 978-1-935786-38-2

Printed in the United States of America and the UK
St. Clair Publications
P. O. Box 726
Mc Minnville, TN 37111-0726

http://stclairpublications.com

Cover Design

Kent Grey-Hesselbein Design Studio
www.kghdesignstudio.com

# Prince Henry St. Clair
# Earl of Orkney

Written and Illustrated by

azel Brown

Edited by Dawn Bramadat

Emma Lynn

Children's Books

# Contents

# safe return

rudging wearily along the heartland, Haakon wanted to ask his grandfather so many questions about the voyage. What had he seen and heard in those lands to the west? Did they find treasure? Had he seen sea monsters?

All his questions would have to wait. The long threatened rain now reached them, falling in torrents. Now they must force their tired legs to hurry on as best they could down the steep muddy track towards the village which had been almost obscured as the evening darkened.

Haakon stopped to rearrange bags and bundles of sea-sodden clothes; icy rain stung his fingers as he heaved the burden onto his shoulders. His grandfather, already weary from his long sea voyage, dragged a heavy basket of tools along the track.

Dark fingers emerged from the rain to meet them. Strong hands took the heavy bags and sturdy arms steadied the old man. A cold wind cut through their wet clothes as they walked in silence towards the welcoming lights shining out from the huddle of houses below.

Haakon's village, an ancient settlement of low, stone crofthouses roofed with turf, had sheltered animals and families alike against the fierce Orkney storms for many generations. The sea supplied a store of fish to dry for winter when the weather was too wild for fishing. The land provided peat for fires, for there were no trees on these rolling islands.

Earlier, on that cold April morning, many of the villagers had seen beacon fires burning brightly across the most distant islands of Orkney. Haakon had been out of his bed and away to call up the small herd of sheep on the hillside above his home, when word reached the village of the sighting of a lone ship bearing the flag of Prince Henry St. Clair.

Haakon watched as the fishermen eagerly put to the sea again in their tiny boats leaving their silver catch along the shore. Small groups of chattering folk were gathering along the cliff edge and there were whispers of excitement on the morning breeze. It was then he heard his mother calling.

"Haakon, Haakon!"

Recognizing the urgency in her voice, Haakon ran swiftly from the sheep and down the rugged hillside, scattering flocks of small birds as he leaped over the low stone wall and down through the heather. On reaching and entering the house he paused, gasping for breath.

"Mother, I'm here. What is it?"

"It's the ship. Earl Henry St. Clair's ship." She took his arm. "Your grandfather, Haakon, he'll be on that ship. They have come home. Run, boy! Down to Kirkwall Bay!" She pushed him gently towards the doorway. Then, holding his arm, she cried, "Wait!"

Brushing across the room, with geese squawking and scattering from under her feet, she found a clean linen cloth, filled it with bread and cheese and handed it to her son. Stuffing the bundle into his shirt, Haakon hurried out of the door and into the bright sunlight.

"I've food to prepare, with no time to do it!" He heard his mother shout after him. "Go boy, run to your grandfather and fetch him home!"

Excitement raced through Haakon's body as he ran from the house, up through the purple heather on the gorse and boulder strewn moor. Reaching the broch at last, he sat on the fallen stones of the ruined Pictish fort, gathering his breath and revelling in the beauty of the place. As the sun warmed his face he could see before him the islands and the glistening sea. Pulling the lunch bundle out of his shirt, he untied the cloth and ate from habit but tasted little for his senses already reeled with anticipation. Suddenly, out of the corner of his eye, he caught sight of the ship.

She was gliding silently between the islands, a beautiful longship. Her sail, bearing the engrailed cross of Prince Henry St. Clair, billowed proudly in the strong westerly wind. Haakon sat spellbound for some time, gazing at the magical sight before him.

The sounding of a horn broke the spell. At that moment he could hardly think or breathe. He ran swiftly down the hillside towards the wide stretch of Kirkwall Bay.

Rain clouds had been gathering from the west as the afternoon drew on, but now seemed to be held back on the blue horizon by the unseen hand of Thor, god of thunder. Gently the ship was guided through Shapinsay Sound, over the tumbling surf and into the protection of the castle at Kirkwall. They were home.

Villagers ran from houses and hillside; men on horses thundered along the shoreline making for the ship with a great blowing of horns and wild shouts. Fishing boats chasing the proud vessel bobbed and danced, their company eager to see the ship's gallant crew.

As Haakon reached the level of the strand, more women and children came tumbling out of their houses leaving cooking pots, screeching hens and barking dogs. Very soon all were caught up in the rush for a fair sighting of the vessel. Mothers held back their children from the rowdy gathering of horses and men busy with ropes and oars. Gulls, curious, yet disturbed by the noisy crowd, screamed overhead.

Haakon squeezed through the throng of people, at times crawling between their legs, attempting to get a clear view.

"Here, let the lad through," said one man, "'tis Harald the blacksmith's grandson."

"Come on, my boy. 'Tis a sight you'll see only once to tell your children."

Haakon was well-grown for his twelve years and could now see Earl Henry standing on the prow of the ship, a tall, broad-shouldered man with red hair to match the great red cloak about his shoulders. The drawn face relaxed with happiness on seeing his men reunited with their families and then his gaze searched the castle windows, eager for a sight of his own wife and children. All at once a cheer went up as the ship touched shore.

A band of men from the castle had appeared; knights wearing white tunics with longswords at their sides: the Templar Knights, friends and kinsmen, were arriving to greet their prince. Among them stood the Venetian, Antonio Zeno, who had sailed westward with Henry two years before. He had returned last September with men eager to be home and close to their families before winter and bringing news of great discoveries.

The crowd on the shore, unable to restrain their excitement and high spirits after their long wait, was calling for Earl Henry now. Two strong men emerged from among them. Surging forwards they swung up onto the bow of the ship and lifted Henry bodily, carrying him shoulder-high over the side of the ship and bearing him aloft through the sea of cheering faces. Old men watched with tears running into their beards and sobbing women reached out to touch their jarl.

As they set him down gently on the quayside Henry stumbled, his sea legs unbalancing him. Immediately many eager hands reached to steady the tall man, but he laughed and eased his body onto a low wall as the crowd closed in around him.

Haakon turned to look at the great longship. The sun was setting rapidly and the late afternoon light was fast fading. Dark rain clouds lay heavily over the far islands and between sky and sea ran a blood-red strip of dying sun. Twilight crept over the distant hills. The vessel was bathed in the glowing light of torches lit by the men unloading a cargo of pelts and barrels; all was still busy and noisy. Then Haakon heard the voice he knew so well.

"Haakon, my boy, give me your arm."

"Grandfather!" Haakon exclaimed, overjoyed to see him but alarmed at the sight of the man. His fair hair had turned to silver. His hollow face and stooped shoulders were proof of a grueling voyage, but his bright blue eyes twinkled with happiness at seeing the boy again—so much taller. Now Haakon felt the welcome warmth of his grandfather's arms around him.

"Come on, lad, help me with my belongings." Harald's voice was hoarse with overpowering emotion.

Gathering up bags and baskets of tools, they set off and came to where the crowd was now moving away, reluctantly leaving the Earl to bid farewell to his crew.

"Come Harald," said Earl Henry as his arm slipped around the tired shoulders of the older man, "We have returned to our islands, to our loved ones. We will remember this day of April, 1400, to tell our children. And we shall keep in our hearts and memory our companion and brave knight, Jamie Gunn, who we buried with his sword and mourned with our tears on that distant shore." Here the surrounding band of men fell silent and bowed their heads respectfully.

Henry then continued on a brighter note, "At Midsummer Solstice we shall have a great feast to celebrate our voyage and our safe homecoming; you and your kin shall all be welcomed to my Hall to share meat and ale. For many days we will tell the stories of our long journey of discovery, but now, my brave men, away to your kinsfolk and your beds!" He laughed heartily as many fond farewells were exchanged.

Large drops of rain began to fall as Haakon and his grandfather gathered up the bags and baskets once more. They made their way out of Kirkwall Bay beyond the quayside and castle towards the headland, and Earl Henry St. Clair was escorted by his knights and kinsmen to the castle and to the reunion with his beloved wife, Janette.

# the sword of sigurd

**n**eighbors eager for news of the return of Harald Haraldsson were gathering in the narrow doorways of their crofthouses, watching the trackway leading to the village. They recognised man and boy approaching, silent and tired, and a woman hastened out of the gloom to call to Haakon's mother, Mathild. Thanking the woman, Mathild hastily left the well-stacked peat fire in her small kitchen, stepped out into the rain-soaked night and ran to her father. Taking his arm, she quickly led the tired old man and her son towards the house and the warm fire.

While the men helped her father out of his wet clothes, Mathild looked to the food and ale. Shivering, Haakon peeled off his dripping shirt. Soon both Harald and Haakon were wrapped in warm, homespun shawls and blankets, and rough, knitted stockings were put on their cold feet. Several of the women helped Mithild to serve out the good, hot food, to satisfy the hunger of the menfolk.

The tiny crofthouse was filled with steaming bodies and excited voices and the warm, sweet smell of the animals that watched silently from the side of the low partition. The smoke-filled kitchen and living room had witnessed many gatherings of kinsfolk for the telling of winter stories on long, cold nights, but this night, Haakon's mother noticed the exhaustion on her father's face, the bright spots of colour in his hollow cheeks. It was sleep that he needed and so she urged her neighbors to return to their homes until her father had rested. Warmly they said their farewells, wishing Harald a peaceful night, and they made their way home.

After closing the door against the wind and the rain, Mathild helped Harald to his bed.

"All the talk can wait till tomorrow," she insisted. Tears were stinging her eyes but she did not want to show the emotion she was feeling. Yet her father knew of her pain and that the relief of his safe return had brought back the memory of her dead husband.

"You're a brave lass," he said, holding her close. "I'm going to stay in my bed now. I'll not give ye any more trouble by being taken with sickness."

Mathild smiled at her father through her tears, feeling secure and strong again. She'd had to be strong for Haakon and for herself for several years now, and when her father had sailed away with Earl Henry it had been another burden of pain to bear. Turning to Haakon, she smiled at the boy.

"Get dressed and quickly put your clogs on, my child," she told him. Take oats to the pony and see that she's settled for the night."

Happy to help his mother, Haakon left the warm kitchen with his grandfather safely in bed and Mathild making up the fire, filling the large iron pot with handfuls of course oats and leaving it to simmer till morning.

Creeping silently out of the house, he stood for a few moments beside the low stone wall facing the sea. The sky was filled with bright stars and the rain had stopped; the night air felt cold and was fragrant on his face. A full moon hung low over the far island of Shapinsay, lighting the way for the fishermen hauling the creels of lobster and crab into their boats. Half dreaming, Haakon sent up his thanks to the round white moon for the safe return of his grandfather, then, swiftly running back to the barn, he crooned to the cattle, telling them about the day's adventure. He tethered the old wooden door and crept softly back to his own small stone bed. The warm straw mattress smelled sweet that night. He could hear his grandfather snoring and he smiled to himself. How good it was to feel the close presence of the old man in their home again.

His thoughts drifted to his father, whose songs had once filled the house and byre. A tall, bright-haired man who he had followed over moor and through peat bogs searching for rabbits and plover's eggs. Many days had been spent chasing sheep, and in the evenings Haakon had listened to his father, spellbound, as he told the old stories of the islands.

Crooning the boy to sleep, he would recite tales of the selkies, the seals with their sad brown eyes and their love of music. Coming ashore on moonlit nights, he told Haakon, they would cast off their skins and dance on the sand in human form.

A man had once watched a sea-girl as she danced and spun in the moonlight. Wanting to own her, he crept up and stole her pelt so that she could not get back into the water to return to her home beneath the waves. She became his wife and drudged for him. After many years had passed, the selkie lass found her lost skin hidden in the loft above the barn and she slipped away in the dead of the night, back to the sea, to her long-lost family and freedom.

Then there were the stories of beautiful children stolen from their homes and taken away to the islands of Suleskerry or Hether Blether, never to be seen again.

Haakon's father had been content as a crooner-fisherman, rowing out to his creels and keeping a few sheep and cows. But the sea did not give freely without taking back her due. She was called the 'widow-maker' amongst the islanders.

One fine spring morning Haakon's father had rowed out to his creels, only to be caught up in a sudden squall on those dangerous waters. He had never returned.

The beaches and coves had been scoured for days, but eventually the men abandoned their search, knowing that the sea had claimed him, she was the provider but also the destroyer; many a young woman had stood on the shore watching and waiting for the sea to return a lost husband or lover.

There were tales told of women who sold favorable winds to fishermen and sailors, wizened old hags who could brew up a storm by just gazing at the sea.

Haakon missed his father and the magical stories, but he knew that life here with his mother and kinsfolk was good. The cows to be milked, the sheep to be gathered in, seasons of storm and ice, summer festivals of fire—all gave him the richness he needed to shape his young life. He dreamed of his father that night, standing beside him on the prow of a great longship.

When Haakon awoke the next morning, Mathild was already up and stirring to life the porridge in the iron pot over the fire.

"Your grandfather was very restless during the night. I fear he may have a fever," she told her son. "Go to the barn and see to the cows and I'll sit with him awhile."

Mathild prepared a healing potion of herbs as Haakon left the croft. The wind had risen again before the dawn, racing down from the north and bringing with it squalls of rain and sleet. The animals were huddled in the barn, listening to the growing gale outside. Haakon milked the cows and ran back to the house, nearly spilling the thick warm liquid in his hurry to be with his grandfather.

Time passed. Mathild sat at her spinning wheel and kept a watchful eye on her restless father. Neighbors called, bringing loaves of freshly-baked bread and herbs to soothe Harald's fever. The day wore on. High winds battered the huddle of crofts; sheets of ice rain poured over the turf roof as mother and son sat patiently waiting for the fever to pass.

Word of Harald's sickness soon reached Earl Henry, and the following morning saw him riding out from Kirkwall accompanied by the Venetian, Antonio Zeno. Both were eager to see their good friend and companion.

Mathild welcomed the two men warmly—honoured guests in her humble home. She bade them both be seated by the fire, then shooing the stray hens from her small kitchen, she hurried to her father and gently woke him with the news of his visitors. Harald slowly opened his eyes while Mathild invited Earl Henry and Sir Antonio to draw close to her father's bedside.

Henry handed the old man a flagon. "Some good red wine to put life back into your veins!" he jested. Harold smiled weakly and thanked the Earl for his kindness. "It is rest and good food that you need," Henry continued more seriously. "Your good daughter's care will have you restored to us very soon."

Mathild left the men to talk and went to the kitchen to fetch oatcakes and ale for their refreshment.

As he returned home, Haakon saw the tethered horses and crept cautiously into the byre and through a little side door into the croft. Hearing the voice of the Earl and not wanting to miss anything, he sat quietly on a low stool beside the partition at the far end of the kitchen.

Haakon noticed that Earl Henry had the same cloak of dark red velvet about his shoulders that he had worn on the prow of the longship. It was held in place by a large pin of knotted silver serpents. Sir Antonio seemed much grander in his tunic of purple velvet, cloak of green and yellow hose and sporting a large feather in his hat. Both men wore longswords at their sides, Haakon was imagining the battles and skirmishes these swords had witnessed when Earl Henry broke into his daydreams, calling the boy to come out of the shadows and join them as Mathild brought food and drink for all.

They ate and talked of many things. The Earl was well known by the islanders to be a fair and generous man, always willing to listen to their worries and difficulties and ever ready with words of advice and encouragement. He delighted, too, in the island stories of the ancient people who had lived in the stone villages, the howes and brochs. He loved to hear of the long-dead ancestors whose bones lay beneath such great burial mounds as Macshowe and he also relished stories of the sea—of whirlpools and mysterious islands, sea serpents and selkies.

But all the talking was making Harald sleepy.

"We must be away, good woman, and let the man have his rest," Henry told Mathild.

Harald thanked the two men again for their kindness while Haakon ran to the barn. Untethering the horses, the boy led them to where the men were exchanging farewells with his mother. Before he mounted his horse, Henry's hand brushed Haakon's head lightly.

"Your grandfather is a brave man," he told the boy. "He saw much hardship on the voyage. Keep him in good cheer and send him to us in good cheer on the feast day of the solstice."

Haakon bowed his head, acknowledging the honour of this responsibility. With trembling fingers, he handed the reins of the horse to the Earl. Mathild softly rested her arm across Haakon's shoulders and watched as the two men galloped away over the rough track towards the high moor.

The wind was high and wild the following day with the sun bursting through racing clouds. Haakon watched the white horses riding over the crashing surf below him as he strolled down across the fields, the warm carcase of a rabbit he had snared tied to his belt—good, nourishing food to take to his grandfather.

On the way he met his cousins, Jon and Eugenie, but told them he could not walk with them that day along the shoreline to look for driftwood and treasures because Jarl Henry St. Clair had commanded him to sit with his grandfather until he was better.

The seriousness in Haakon's voice impressed his cousins and they both nodded with understanding, watching silently as he walked on home.

Haakon handed the rabbit to his mother.

"For Grandfather," he announced proudly and turned to take off his tunic and clogs.

Harold was feeling brighter this morning and smiled warmly at the boy.

"Thank you, Haakon," he said. "Neighbor Ericsson brought vegetables in for us not a half hour ago, so he must have guessed you would be coming home with a young rabbit in your belt. What a feast we shall have!"

When Haakon had finished his tasks, he sat with his grandfather for the rest of the day. So began many happy days spent in each other's company. Harald, cheered by his grandson's willing presence, drew with words many pictures of the sights he had seen and of his life on the islands of Orkney. But Haakon was eager to hear exactly how his grand-

father had become blacksmith and armourer to Earl Henry St. Clair and about their great sea voyage.

"Well," pondered Harald, "I shall start at the beginning, lad." He pulled a warm blanket closer to him. "When I was a boy, I watched my father and grandfather working with the horses and making iron ploughs in the spitting fires of the forge. Many horses were brought for my father to shoe. That is why the island is called 'Hrossey', meaning 'The Island of the Horse', for without the labor of horses, oxen and plough, these islands would still be wild and untamed.

Just as your father used his creels to work in the sea, my father worked with the iron and the fire and so the wild uplands were put to the plough. After I had learned my forefathers' trade, I went to work at my father's forge and soon I travelled out of the islands, repairing ploughs."

Fascinated, Haakon watched his grandfather's face closely. The man had a far-off look about his eyes as he recalled those long-ago times.

"It was not until about the year 1380 that I met Earl Henry, newly come to these islands as our Jarl with his young wife, Janette, and their pretty children. He had need of men to build his fortress at Kirkwall and that is how we met. A good bond was struck between us and it has stood the test to this day." Harald paused, seeing in his mind the passing of those years.

"Where did Jarl Henry live before he came here to Kirkwall, Grandfather?" asked Haakon, gently drawing Harald into the present.

"Well, boy, Earl Henry told me many stories of his young life. He once lived in a fine castle near Edinburgh to the south. A castle called Rosslyn—a grand place. The building was begun in the year 1304 by Earl Henry's ancestors. It is not to be found on a high hill as you might expect, but in a wooded valley, snug against the winter winds."

"Could it not be easily attacked in such a position?" asked Haakon, surprised.

"No, son, for it towers above its near surroundings and is too far from the valley slopes to be battered or attacked. Indeed, two sides are protected by wide river marshes." The man's eyes gleamed as he warmed to the subject. "Aye, that castle has thick walls, a strong beacon tower, a barbican, a causeway, a bridge, drawbridge and portcullis—'tis a grand sight, Haakon."

Encouraged by his grandson's unwavering attention, Harald readily went on to describe the Great Hall which was hung with rich tapestries worked in silks and many brilliant colours and interwoven with threads of gold—a long room with a raised platform upon which stood a tall, carved chair.

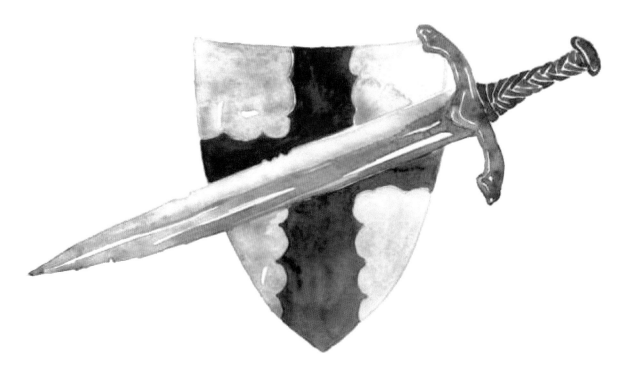

"Above a huge fireplace hung a great two-edged sword—the sword of Sigurd the Sea-King, second Earl of Orkney who was born in 871. He was the brother of Rognvald the Mighty, first Jarl of Orkney. Now, Haakon, as a boy Earl Henry often gazed up at the sword. It was, he told me, as if some ancient magic had been folded into its scarred blade. When he was a young man he lifted it down from its resting place; feeling, with reverence he said, the blade dented by many battles. He vowed then always to keep it with him both as a talisman and to remind him of his ancestors and their Viking blood. The sword is now at Kirkwall. I will show it to you one day when I take you to the Hall."

Many vivid pictures flashed through Haakon's mind as he imagined the sword of Sigurd, the grand castle of Rosslyn and its battlements, the Great Hall… Harold's voice broke into the boy's thoughts.

"You know," he continued, "Earl Henry's father was a canny man. He invented a contraption of wood and pulleys that could haul the food up from the kitchens below through holes in the floors to the Great Hall at the top of the castle. There were many feasts and happy gatherings in those days; tournaments in the field and hunting on the Pentland Hills.

"It was a large family with many kith and kin—a lineage of both Norman and Viking blood."

"How so, Grandfather?" Haakon asked.

"Well, Rognavald the Mighty had many sons. The second son, Hrolf, married a lady called Gisselle, daughter of Charles the Simple, King of France, and so he was granted the lands of Normandy by a treaty signed at St. Clair-sur-Epte in the year 912. The place had taken its name from the hermit, Saint Clair, and as the family had lived there they took the name St. Clair. The St. Clairs were cousins to William the Conqueror; nine of Earl Henry's ancestors fought in the battle of Hastings."

Haakon's eyes lit up again. His father had once told him of this great battle. Encouraged, Harald continued.

"You see, one of Henry's forebears, a man called William the Seemly St. Clair, had been granted the Barony of Rosslyn and Pentland by Malcolm Canmore. In his youth, William had been attached to the Atheling family and had accompanied Edgar the Atheling to Hungary. He returned to Scotland with Edgar's sister, Margaret, in 1057 with part of the true Cross—the Holy Rood. Margaret married King Malcolm Canmore and William became her cupbearer. Yet another ancestor and namesake of Henry, Henri de St. Clair, fought beside Godfroi de Bouillon during the first Crusade in Jerusalem in 1096.

"Several St. Clairs became Knights Templar and the St. Clair lands in Scotland became a Templar refuge when the Pope took it upon himself to torture and kill those knights who had been to the Holy Land. They fled from France and were taken in by their kinsmen in Scotland."

His head reeling with all those long-dead warriors, Haakon wanted to know exactly where their present Earl fitted in.

"Henry," Harald explained, "was the first-born of Sir William and Lady Isabella, daughter of Malise Sparre, Earl of Orkney. Before Henry was born, Malise Sparre died, leaving Isabella heir to the Jarldom of Orkney. She eventually passed it down to Henry, but, he has told me, not without many difficulties.

"He was born in the year 1345 in the Robin Hood tower at Rosslyn Castle. Sir William carried him straight away to St. Matthew's church to be baptized just in case he should die suddenly, for the plague wiped out thousands of people in those days. A few years later, when he was quite seriously sick, he was given the special waters of the Balm Well."

"What kind of special water was that?" asked Haakon.

"A sort of oily water said to have healing powers from the precious bones of their patron, St. Katherine. Whatever it was, he told me it saved him.

Both man and boy were silent for a moment. The plague had taken many lives in Scotland and there was always the fear of it reaching the islands. But Haakon's thoughts soon turned to Henry's boyhood again.

"What did he do at the castle when he was my age?" he persisted.

"He had to learn books and Latin and poetry. There was no milking cows or tending newborn lambs for Henry!" At this, Haakon's grandfather laughed, then explained, "He was trained in the skills of bow and sword. Table manners, too! How to hold his head and bear himself well to be the future Lord of Rosslyn. He had to wash his hands before coming to the table and walk upright at an easy pace, not gobble his food like a goose and run in all directions as you and your cousins do!"

Mathild interrupted their laughter with food and a scolding.

"Don't keep him talking too long Haakon—he must rest now."

But Haakon guessed that since his grandfather had actually begun to

recount all the fine stories of Earl Henry St. Clair, there would be no stopping him. He was brighter in himself, with more life in his old bones now his fever had passed. As they prepared for bed, Haakon longed for the morrow, thinking of the many questions he would ask his grandfather.

*****

Haakon's two cousins, Jon and Eugenie, came bounding into the crofthouse the next morning to visit Harald. They carried between them a wicker creel of freshly caught fish, sent from their father. Haakon was pleased to see his cousins and began excitedly to tell them of the stories of castles, knights and battles he had heard from Harald the previous day.

"Go on! Go on!" the cousins urged Haakon as he came to the end of all he'd been told.

Harald, who had been dozing in his chair by the fire, rearranged his woolen blanket, telling the children to shush their din and sit quiet if they wanted to hear more. So it was that when Mathild returned to the smokey kitchen from her chores outside, she found all three children huddled together in complete silence. They sat still, entranced by Harald's spellbinding stories about a man whose life was so very different from their own. She glanced disapprovingly at the children, yet half-listened, as she had done the day before, to the tale her father was recounting.

After a while the old man paused, gazing intently into the fire as if searching for scenes from the past which would lead the children deeper into the magical world he wished to share with them. When he had been silent for some time, Eugenie urged, "Go on, Granddad Harald!" wanting more of the grand parties and pretty weddings.

"Well, you see, Henry's young days were suddenly cut short. When he was only thirteen years of age, just a year older than you Haakon, his father, Sir William, went to Prussia to join a great crusade. He went to fight in armour with the Teutonic Knights against the infidels who denied the faith of the true Cross. The King of England had captured King David II of Scotland in an invasion, and Sir William, a brave and gallant knight, had hired his men and himself out to raise the huge ransom demanded in exchange for his King.

"So it was that William, together with several lords, each with sixty horsemen and many foot-soldiers were granted safe conduct through England on their way to Prussia.

"The plague had taken a heavy toll throughout Europe and wars in German lands had killed many knights. Henry and his mother watched proudly as Sir William and his men rode away from Rosslyn, but it was not many months before news reached them of Sir William's death. The shock fell very hard upon the whole family, but perhaps hardest on young Henry who was suddenly called to shoulder his father's responsibilities at such an early age."

Haakon thought of the death of his own father and of how he had had to fill the role of the man of the house while Grandfather was away.

Harold went on, "He told me how becoming Lord of Rosslyn," Harald went on, "took the fun out of his young life. He sought advice from his uncles and his mother, the Lady Isabella. She was a powerful woman, always willing to help her son, and later she won him the Earldom of Orkney. His father, too, had taught him well and this knowledge gave Henry the strength he needed to take over the Barony of Rosslyn. He studied law and politics, preparing himself for his future as Jarl of Orkney. Then, at the age of twenty-one, he received a knighthood and became Sir Henry St. Clair."

In the warmth of the fire Eugenie had fallen asleep, but Haakon and Jon hung on every word Harald spoke as the life of the man at Kirkwall unfolded before them.

"Were there any more battles?" asked Jon.

"Well, Earl Henry spoke often about his forebears, and one in particular, Sir Henri St. Clair, who in 1314 led the Knights Templar at the Battle of Bannockburn. This Sir Henri had married Alicia, daughter of Ramsay of Dalhousie, and it was their son, William St. Clair, together with his brother John and Sir James Douglas, who traveled to Palestine with the heart of Robert the Bruce in 1330. Then suddenly, in an encounter with the Moors in Spain, they lost their lives and their poor dead bodies were brought back to Scotland.

The boys wished to know much more of the battles and longswords, but now Eugenie awoke and asked if Earl Henry had had a sweetheart, and did his sisters wear beautiful gowns. She didn't want to hear all about those long-dead heroes.

"Aye, lass," replied Harald, "he had a sweetheart."

The boys groaned, but Harald went on. "Earl Henry's boyhood companion was Jamie Gunn. As boys, they had galloped their horses over the hills and danced with all the pretty ladies at the castle, yet, right from his early childhood, Henry tells me, he always knew he loved Janette Halyburton, the daughter of the Lord of Dirleton Castle. In 1353 a marriage was arranged between Henry and Princess Florentina, however the princess died before she was of marriageable age, so Henry was free to return to his childhood sweetheart, Janette. Henry loved Janette and didn't believe in the idea of arranged marriages that was the usual procedure in such grand families then. He courted Janette, spoke to her father, and they were married when she was just fifteen and he was seventeen."

Eugenie's romantic curiosity was still not satisfied. She wanted to hear more. She climbed down from Harald's chair and sat with her aunt, picking up the threads from the floor under the spinning wheel.

"Is the Earl's wife a fine lady?" she asked.

"She is as pretty now as when they both met," her aunt put in, "and more than likely it was a fancy wedding, with dainty gowns and a feast to remember."

Harald smiled. "It wasn't long after their marriage that she bore him a son and they named him Henry, after his father. Later Janette gave him four more sons and nine daughters. She had in attendance upon her fifty-five gentlewomen, thirty-five of them being Ladies, and Earl Henry himself had three hundred riding gentlemen. His power and estate, and that of his son Henry, were considerable. He was a busy man who had to visit kings and queens in foreign countries and at home, and attend the Scottish Parliament at Scone. Indeed, he was requested to sail to Denmark to attend the wedding of Princess Margaret and King Haakon."

"He had my name!" cried Haakon, pleased.

"His brother, John, married Princess Eugenie of Denmark, thus securing the link between the two countries," Harald went on.

"And I'm named after a real princess!" put in Eugenie.

Jon urged them both to be quiet and let their grandfather finish his story.

"Well, now he is our Jarl, living with his good lady at Kirkwall, confirmed as Earl of Orkney on the 2nd day of August in the year 1379 and charged to protect these islands and to give allegiance to Queen Margaret of Norway."

Harald rose from his chair and stretched his arms above his head. "And that is how I met Earl Henry and became blacksmith and armourer at the castle. Now away with you all and leave me in peace to sup my ale."

The children were slow to move. Their heads had been filled with visions of chivalry and splendor, knights and battles, kings and princesses. There was enough to fill their dreams for many a long night.

As if to break the spell, Mathild put away her wool and wheel, lighting the fish-oil lamps before she prepared supper. The afternoon had vanished.

# shipwreck

harp, salty winds blew in from the Atlantic. Clouds swirled across the blue sky like billowing smoke. Haakon had climbed the craggy outcrop of rock along the cliffs looking for stray sheep. The wide sweep of sea and sky stretched above and beneath him. He was unable to hear anything over the howling wind, but his eye suddenly caught a movement far below in the cave.

Several men were running towards a cluster of rocks that sprawled just beyond his vision. He scrambled quickly onto a high, grassy hillock and saw a ship below him, lurching precariously through the crashing waves. She seemed to be held one minute, then thrown mercilessly against the treacherous rocks the next. Her sails in tatters, she was battered again and again by the pounding surf. Horrified, Haakon watched as the ship's crew clung to ropes and spars. Half-drowned and filled with terror, they shouted frantically to the men on the shore.

Haakon clutched at the coarse, wet grass beneath his fingers. He felt helpless — too far from the beach below to reach them in time to help. It was almost unbearable to watch the scene. He held his breath as some men on the beach threw a rope to the ship and others dived into the roaring sea. The sailors caught the rope and clung onto it bravely, flinging themselves into the crashing foam to be brought to the safety of the shore.

By this time the crowd of onlookers had swelled and more people were running along the shore towards the stricken crew. All watched helplessly as the little ship broke up, throwing crates and barrels in every direction. The islanders salvaged what they could for the poor sailors, leaving the rest to be washed ashore on the incoming tide. `

Soon the shipwrecked crewmen were gathered together and gently escorted to the shelter of the village. Meanwhile, Haakon, his thoughts racing, ran all the way home with the news of the wreck.

"'Tis not a rare thing around these islands," Harald said on hearing his grandson's tale. "The bones of many ships and men have come aground in the treacherous waters of our bays. Indeed, I witnessed one shipwreck that was to change all our lives."

With the excitement of the morning's adventure still fresh in his mind, Haakon wanted more stories of wrecks. His mother had gone up to the pasture to bring in the cows and he knew there would be time to sit with his grandfather before she returned and his chores must be done.

"We were away up to the wild islands off Shetland with Earl Henry," Harald began readily. "He wished to make himself known to his people, among whom he included the isolated folk, ancient, dark, and believed by some to be creatures of the night, who lived with the dwarves and faerie folk on those windswept islands.

"We had left our ship at Bressay, and wild it was, with the sky dark, and threatening rain. We made fast our boat and headed for the priest's house. Earl Henry said he would make himself known and find shelter for us there, but all we found were a few ruined hovels. We made a rough camp and as the weather worsened, old Thorfin Johnsson said he would go and check that our boat was made fast against the incoming tide.

"Before long he came running back shouting, 'Ship on the rocks!' and then ran off to the priest's hovel to call Earl Henry. The sight that met our eyes when we reached the shore was one I'll never forget, lad—the most savage horde of men and women I've ever yet beheld. Wild-haired, dirty and ragged, armed with long knives and spears, they were not going to allow any of us to reach the stricken ship. This was their prize.

"Earl Henry soon joined us, standing tall with a drawn sword in his hand. 'Stand aside,' he ordered, shouting to the ragged warriors, but they stood their ground, pointing weapons and fists menacingly in our direction. 'You are all murdering heathens!' roared Henry, for it was clear that they were all ready to cut the throats of every poor sailor aboard the desperate vessel. 'Harm any one of those men and we'll cut you down,' Henry told them fearlessly, 'I am your Jarl, Henry St. Clair, and I will witness no slaughter here this night. Stand aside!'"

"And they did?" broke in Haakon, wide-eyed.

"Every one of them," replied Harald with satisfaction.

"But what of the ship, Grandfather? Did it crash onto the rocks?"

"Aye, but we got a line to her and brought every man safely to shore. When we heard Earl Henry greeting the olive-skinned captain, we found out that it was the ship of Nicolo Zeno, a man Earl Henry had met in Venice and the brother of Carlo Zeno of the Zeno family.

"You see, when Earl Henry accompanied King Peter of Cyprus and his chancellor, Philip de Mezieres, to Copenhagen in 1364 to raise forces and funds for a new crusade, he met Carlo Zeno there. Carlo invited Henry and many of his Scottish knights to visit Venice and to meet his family. He wished to show them the Grand Arsenal and the great Venetian fleet. Henry was extremely impressed with the fine shipbuilding and the navigational skills of the Venetian sailors and so invited Carlo's brother, Nicolo, to sail to Orkney as the guest of himself and his family.

"On his voyage to our islands to meet Prince Zichmi, as Nicolo called Henry, his ship went off course and got into difficulties, but, as I've told you, luckily sailed right into our hands and safety."

"Who was Carlo Zeno, Grandfather? What did he do?" asked Haakon, still hungry for more details.

"What did he do! He only saved Venice from the Genoese!" Harald responded enthusiastically.

"Who were the Genoese?" Haakon was still puzzled.

"The Genoese, armed with men, mortars and bombards, blockaded the city of Venice. Many urgent messages requesting immediate help were sent to Captain Carlo, who was away in the Mediterranean with all the armed galleys, but no reply came.

"Supplies ran low and the poor people of Venice faced starvation. The Doge and Council were in despair and reluctantly announced that the city would have to surrender by New Year's Day unless the fleet returned. On that very day, the first of the year in 1381, Carlo Zeno was sighted with fifteen armed galleys laden with provisions. He attacked the Genoese at Choggia and forced them to surrender. Grandly rewarded by the grateful citizens of Venice, he became Admiral of the Fleet and was renamed 'Carlo the Dragon'."

Haakon's excitement rose as he remembered that Sir Antonio Zeno, Carlo's older brother, had come to visit his grandfather with Earl Henry and had sat in this very room.

"So you see," Harald explained, "we had saved the life of a very famous man that day on Fer Island. There and then, Earl Henry invited Nicolo Zeno and his crew to sail back to Kirkwall with us and to make it his home for as long as he wished."

Harald went on to tell Haakon of the wonderful things Nicolo had brought with him on his voyage. Among the many precious items saved from the wreck were maps and instruments of navigation.

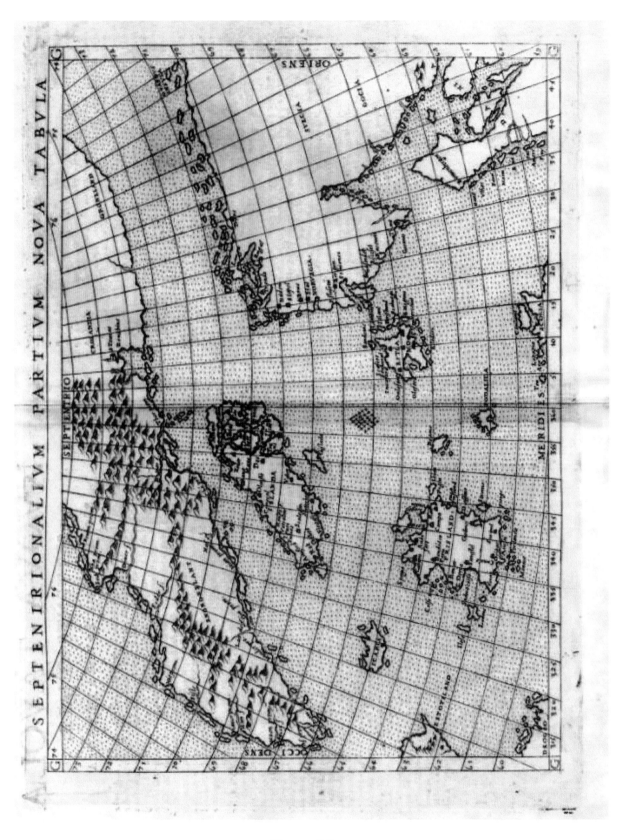

**Zeno Map**

"In his castle at Kirkwall, Earl Henry eagerly studied the maps spread before him as Nicolo and his men pointed out lands yet uncharted. Henry then invited the Templar Knights to fetch what maps and charts were in their possession and, with papers spread across the room, many a long day was spent in deep discussion. From the start there was much eager talk of taking a fleet of ships, well-provisioned, to search out new lands.

"I remember that Earl Henry spoke of sailing to an island that existed far to the west. It was fertile, he said—rich in gold and with great timber forests. But to do this, ships were needed. He said he had heard of an old fisherman, now living in Kirkwall, who some years earlier had sailed away from Orkney to fish for cod, but was tossed in the wild ocean, only to be washed ashore on this very island."

Here Harald paused, rose from his seat to stretch his stiff limbs, and putting fresh peat upon the fire, said to Haakon, "Your mother will be here soon, my lad, and you've chores to do." He poured himself some ale.

Haakon wanted very much to hear more about the old fisherman and pleaded with his grandfather to continue his story.

"Well, if you finish your chores, son, and let an old man have his nap, there'll be time after supper to hear the rest." And with that, Haakon had to be content.

# the fisherman's tale

For many centuries, men from the islands of Orkney had ventured far without compass or map into the vast ocean of the Atlantic, some chasing shoals of silver herring westwards to seek out the lands of legend towards the setting sun.

In frail curraghs or sleek longships, many were drawn towards that vast limitless ocean and its magic. Tales were told and retold of distant ancestors and lands to the west—islands filled with good timber forests, lakes of fresh water, strange animals, birds of many colours and delicious fruits and vines.

Harald assured his grandson that to recount all the stories of the Norsemen and their discoveries would take many winter nights. He must content himself for the moment with the tale of the old fisherman. So Haakon settled beside his mother as she sat spinning and both listened in silence as the story unfolded.

"About six and twenty years ago, a fisherman set out from these islands with many men in four boats. They sailed for several days to their fishing grounds but were suddenly caught up in a violent storm, far from land. For days they were tossed by heavy seas and battered by strong winds. One boat was overturned in the raging sea and the crewmen were rescued by their companions in the other three boats. They clung in fear to the small craft and prayed for their lives.

"When the storm abated after many long days and nights, the men found themselves washed up on a strange shore a thousand miles from home. No sooner had they made for dry land than they were set upon by the native inhabitants of that place. They were made captive and taken to a fair city where they were brought before the King, but neither party could speak the other's language.

"The King called for an interpreter, a monk of Irish descent who had lived on the island for many years. He spoke and understood both Latin and the language of the King. The native people, he explained, wanted the fishermen to stay, and were prepared to oblige them to do so by force rather than persuasion. So, as the fishermen could find no means to escape, they contented themselves with their new-found home which was, the old monk told them, named Estotiland.

In time, the fishermen were able to explore many parts of the island and they soon realised that it was a very fertile place, not wild and untamed as their own homeland had once been. It was naturally rich in timber, and meat and fish were plentiful, as were fruits and vines. The climate was mild and they passed their days in captivity in warm sunshine.

"After five years, the King decided to send the fishermen south to another island, so once more they set sail with generous provisions, only to be set upon yet again by rough weather which sent them off course. Their little boat soon struck rocks in the fierce storm and was washed ashore, where, at dawn, they found themselves on another strange island, surrounded by a race of wild people wearing only skins for clothes.

"Again they were taken captive and watched closely at first, but the native people soon found the unfortunate fishermen to be quite harmless and became friendly with them. The old fisherman studied the people and their customs carefully, and soon noticed that their method of fishing was fairly primitive and clumsy. Whenever he was given any freedom he spent his time scouring the island, finding materials suitable to his task. He then proceeded to show the native people how to make strong nets and use hand lines. These were magical wonders to the natives who, excited by their new tools, allowed the old fisherman to roam freely about the island. But although the land was beautiful and the food plentiful, the fisherman wished only for his home and family after so many years spent among these very different people.

"Waiting until the time was right, he slipped silently away, and guided by the light of the moon, he made his way down the coast. He stopped to rest just before dawn, having already travelled many miles. Looking out to sea, he saw a ship lying in the calm waters of a bay. Without hesitating, he dived into the sea and swam towards her, calling out to the mariners on board in his own language. The seamen pulled him aboard, surprised by his unexpected and ragged appearance. They gave him fresh clothes and food, as he ate, he told them about his adventures.

"The ship, it turned out, had been blown off course and was now bound for the Faroe Islands. The captain and crew flatly refused to attempt to rescue his fellow-fishermen, saying that it would mean certain death for them all, but promised gladly to return the fisherman to his homeland of Orkney."

Haakon drew a deep breath as his grandfather finished the tale.

"Did you know the man, Grandfather?" he asked.

"Aye, I knew the man. His family had given him up for dead, so you can imagine how they rejoiced at his return. When Earl Henry heard the story of the old fisherman himself, he wanted to know how those lands could be found again. The old man told the Earl everything he knew, repeating his story many times and saying that he never wished to put to sea again. But Earl Henry had plans to make the voyage for himself and begged the old man to sail with him."

Haakon climbed into bed that night and lay listening to the cattle lowing in the byre. He would not want to be away from his home and family, he thought, to be swept by tides and winds to some far-off shore. He felt safe at home with his mother and Harald. Hearing the wind rising, he pulled the warm blanket thankfully over his head and soon drifted off to sleep.

At daybreak the crowing cock rudely brought Haakon back to reality from a night of dreams. Tattered sails on battered ships and drifting islands had filled his slumbers. The morning being fair with mild breezes, the sun's warmth drew folk from their smokey crofts to spend a little time in exchanging gossip. A dog snoozed under the shade of a wall. Whispers of warm weather brought promises of repose; a time to take breath and relax for a moment before the harvest was gathered.

Harald strolled with his grandson this fine morning along the shore. They watched silently as a pair of otters dived and swirled in the shallow tide. Several ewes with young lambs had wandered onto the beach and were feeding on the seaweed strewn along the rocks. Sheep were allowed to wander at will on the islands, and so were often found stranded, cut off by the tide or stuck fast in the peat bogs.

Feeling stronger, Harald had decided to help Haakon gather the few stragglers, keeping them well away from the dangerous rocks. Now the ewes seemed content not to stray, so grandfather and grandson found a grassy bank where they could relax awhile and enjoy the warm sunshine.

Gulls wheeled graciously above them in the blue sky. Haakon closed his eyes against the bright light, thinking all the time of the stories his grandfather had told him.

"What happened to Nicolo Zeno after his ship was wrecked?" he asked. "Did he go back to Venice?"

"Well, there's a sad tale to be told there, lad," replied Harald, resting his head back on his hands. "Nicolo Zeno stayed at Kirkwall with Henry for some time, exchanging stories of sea voyages. He had brought new knowledge with him and Earl Henry found him a valuable companion. The Earl respected Sir Nicolo's skills and asked him to become the captain of his small fleet. In the year 1390, Earl Henry built a castle at Bressey in Shetland from where he could set sail on his voyages of discovery. Then, in 1392, after claiming the Faroe Islands on behalf of Queen Margaret of Norway, he obtained special permission to travel to London to purchase two ships that he needed to reinforce his fleet.

"I stayed here at Kirkwall to work under the watchful eye of Sir Nicolo. He taught me his knowledge of weaponry, showing me, for example, how to cast the latest type of cannon that was loaded from the muzzle and had a small breech for setting the charge. Harald's voice was warm with genuine admiration. "He knew how the recoil of a ship's cannon could be resisted by having two iron pivots, or trunnions firmly lashed to ringbolts in the deck. These also provided a means of swiveling or turning and aiming the cannon without maneuvering the ship. At that time, Nicolo's brother, Antonio Zeno, was also living in Orkney. He had brought with him the latest Venetian galley, equipped with crew and cannon, and we all worked closely together to perfect Earl Henry's armoury.

"Earl Henry had other plans for Sir Nicolo, too. In 1393 he sent him with a flotilla of four ships to carry out a survey of Greenland and, at the same time, to arrange an exchange of bishops between Orkney and Greenland."

Harald paused, complaining that he was famished with all the talking. Haakon took out bread, cheese and ale from a small bag and both of them sat under the midday sun, satisfying their hunger and quenching their thirst. Gulls eager for a stray morsel flew close, alighting on the nearby rocks.

Now Harald continued, supping the cool ale. "Sir Nicolo returned from Greenland in a sorry state. Too much exposure to snow and ice had made him sickly and weak."

Haakon looked out to sea, remembering other stories he had heard from his father—stories of the fire and ice, wastelands of snow and savage Skaelings. He wouldn't have been in Sir Nicolo's shoes for anything!

"He brought back news of a monastery he'd come across, built close to a hill that spouted fire like Vesuvius and Etna, and where hot water bubbled up from beneath the ground.

"The monastery was run by the Order of Friars—preachers with a church dedicated to Saint Thomas. The Black Friars welcomed Sir Nicolo and he saw how they used the hot water from the springs under the ground to heat their halls and cook their food. He charted the position of the monastery and sailed the length and breadth of the coast of Greenland.

"Aye, it's a strange land, son, haunted by trolls and demons and peopled by wild men. Sir Nicolo met savage hunters and fishermen who traded in dried fish and animal skins. He was excited by their use of small boats in the treacherous storms that plagued those freezing shores. But, all in all, the voyage proved too much for the poor man. The severe cold had gotten into his very soul and it was not long before he perished, leaving a great sadness at Kirkwall at the loss of such a courageous man."

Having finished their meal, the man and boy raised themselves from the grassy bank and strolled down to the tideline. Haakon gathered pieces of sun-bleached driftwood, imagining that they had floated ashore from far-off islands—lands of deep forests inhabited by frost giants and trolls. Or perhaps the wood had been blown by winds from the far paradise called 'Mag Mell', an island in a blue sea peopled by faerie folk who preserved the wisdom of the ancestors. Many heroic men had sailed to that golden kingdom, never to be heard of again.

Dropping the driftwood into his bag, Haakon ran over to his grandfather's side.

"Come, boy, your mother will be sending out the search men if we don't start back home!" Harald chuckled. He was feeling so much stronger in himself now; Haakon sensed this as he ran along happily beside his grandfather. Ewes and lambs gathered up ahead and Haakon whistled cheerfully, pushing the sheep along the track, slowly making their way towards the homestead. They had spent such a fine, happy day together.

These early summer days saw all the children eager to be awake at cock crow and heading for the open moor, where they hoped to cut the peat banks. The mornings were spent gathering limpets and mussels, or fishing along the calm, blue shoreline. Larks hung high on the breeze, singing their hearts out. When work was done, the crofters would gather to sit together awhile in the cool evenings, listening to the kin-redders recounting tales and bringing life again to their long-dead ancestors. Fathers, brothers, uncles—all would file past to be presented to the awestruck listeners. Songs would be sung and much ale consumed.

∎∙∙∙∙∙∙∙∙∙∙∙∙∙∙∙∙∙∙∙∙∙∙∙∙∙∙∙∙∙∙∙∙∙∙∙∙∙∙∙∙∙∙∙∙∙∙∙∙∙∙∙∙∙∙∙∙∙∙∙∙∙∙∎

One early June morning found Haakon and his grandfather walking the rough track that led to Kirkwall. Haakon's cousin, Jon, accompanied them and both boys were full of anticipation, sensing an adventure in the air. Scented yellow gorse brushed their legs and the peaty earth was dry beneath their bare feet. All around them the sea laid silver calm in the bay. Harald had promised them this special day. He led the pony, a small sheltie, loaded with produce to sell at the market. The boys' excitement made them chatter all the way to Kirkwall.

Harald smiled and thought himself a lucky man. He had never really considered himself to be religious. He was aware of the seasons and their

changing moods. And yet, there was more: adapting to the dread of winter sometimes made him think of the old gods and the circle of stones at Brodgar. Then the midwinter flash of sunlight through the great burial mound of Maeshowe told him spring would come again to warm the land and bring new life. Indeed, the sun, plucked from winter's icy grip, strengthened in the sky each day. He had certainly prayed unashamedly many times during the long sea voyage, when the ship had been in danger of foundering on those black, storm-lashed nights. Remembering these things, Harald decided to show the boys, after they had finished their business at the market, the great cathedral of Saint Magnus, with its chalice, paten and candlesticks, all of fine silver.

The hustle and bustle of the town was in strong contrast to the quiet of the little croft they had left behind. There was so much to see; ships lying at anchor in the bay waiting to be unloaded; ponies and carts carrying cargo from the quayside; the stalls in the marketplace, laden with dried fish and fresh bread, and overshadowed by the towering cathedral. A man called to them to come try on the clogs he was finishing, while a swarthy old woman with a torn cloak about her shoulders stood behind a stall overflowing with bundles of flax and grubby fleeces. Jon leapt as a ragged dog barked at him from beneath the stall. The smell of the place seemed sour and rotten to Haakon, who was used to the sweet smells of peat smoke and cattle. His grandfather exchanged a bag of dried fish for the goods he needed while the boys investigated every stall, alleyway and dark corner of the marketplace.

By noon, the air, mixed with the smoke from braziers, rotting fish, dust and the general heat of the day, had become stifling. Harald suggested finding a shady wall where they could sit to eat, but the boys preferred the shore and dragged their grandfather to a quiet stretch of the beach. The water was cool between their toes and the breeze from the sea refreshed them after the stuffy marketplace.

The three sat, eating in silence. Harald handed each of the boys an apple. He was not a town or city person—he loved the open moor and the smell of the sea above all things.

"Father told me once that a castle has always stood on that spot," said Jon, nodding towards Earl Henry's stronghold.

"Aye, he's right, son. An ancient ruined castle once stood there, built by a Norseman long ago. Earl Henry used its very foundations upon which to build his new castle. He needed a fortress, but also a home for his wife and children. It had to be strong—a symbol of authority to house soldiers who held themselves in readiness to defend his two hundred islands to the north. An arsenal for weapons, it gives safe cover to the mooring ships. Those ancient foundations, built of solid stone, lie beneath the water, and that arched water entrance is used for loading and unloading the ships you can see entering the waterway."

The castle was surrounded on three sides by the water of the bay. On the land side there was a moat-like channel over which a drawbridge towered. Jon and Haakon gazed up at the great bastion of stone, such a giant compared with their own small crofthouses.

"Hidden within those thick walls," their grandfather explained to the boys, "are the barrack rooms to house the soldiers."

"And secret chambers," Haakon added, almost under his breath.

"Are there secret chambers?" asked Jon hopefully.

"Well if I knew I couldn't tell because they're secret!" laughed Harald.

The two boys smiled but remained silent, momentarily dwelling on the tales they had heard of Viking raids and great hoards of treasure hidden deep within the dungeons of old castles. In them, caves with damp, gloomy tunnels led to vast caverns strewn with the bones of warriors and caskets of gold.

Harald guessed what they were thinking and broke the silence. "Earl Henry wasn't as much concerned with secret tunnels as he was with ships. These were treasures indeed, lads. You can't defend an island with chests of gold unless you put the gold to good use to buy timber and build ships. With the timber he purchased and oak from the forests in the Pentland Hills, Earl Henry was able to put good men to work: shipwrights, carpenters, sailmakers, smiths—myself included. We all had a job to do—build a fleet!"

All three turned their eyes towards the ships lying peacefully at anchor in Kirkwall Bay. The docked Venetian ship of Antonio Zeno lay proudly in the water and a scattering of undocked row boats bobbed alongside.

"A tall, straight oak will make one strong keel and yet another, with a tall trunk which has grown with good curvature, will be used for the prow stem. Another straight oak is needed for a stern post and still another curved oak for the ribs," explained Harald.

Haakon and Jon had watched Jon's father at the shipyard many times, working the great felled oaks. A party of men using axes split the oak down the middle, trimming the sections with axe and adze. They did the same to make the overlapping planks. These were fastened with iron clinch nails. The ships they built were long, squat vessels with a single mast and sails made of coarse linen cloth called wadmal that was strengthened with straps of leather. Finally, wood carvers would decorate the ships with dragon heads and elaborate knotwork.

"Earl Henry built skieds and knorrs," Harold continued. "These sturdier vessels with high freeboards can carry large amounts of cargo and farm animals on open seas. At fifty to a hundred feet in length, some of them are capable of carrying sixty men and a cargo of three hundred tons."

"Tell us now about your voyage with Earl Henry, Grandfather," pleaded Haakon.

"There is no time to be telling you now, my boy. We must be getting back soon, but we'll go to the cathedral before we head for home." Harald got to his feet. He had enjoyed the company of his two grandsons and was proud of their eagerness and enthusiasm.

Before long, they found themselves back at the marketplace. Now deserted by the weary traders, it had taken on a different mood: sullen and empty. The great cathedral towered above them, red sandstone glowing in the afternoon light. Coming to the massive wooden door, Harald halted the boys as if wanting to prepare them to cross the sacred threshold. Silently, they entered the vast sanctuary.

"I can't see anything at all," Haakon whispered.

"Hush, boy, your eyes will soon get used to the dark," Harold told him softly, guiding the two boys down the dimly-lit aisle. Two pale lamps hung from the lofty interior, their soft glow enabling the group to glimpse shapes and colours which gave a promise of something half-obscured.

Having heard their voices, a priest appeared and gently greeted them. Harold whispered a few words to the old man, who then went off into the dark vestry to reappear a moment later with a tall candle.

"Who is this?" Haakon eventually enquired, peering into the gloom.

"And this man with the longsword?" put in Jon.

Gently answering their questions, the priest led the two awestruck boys onwards to gape and stare in wonderment at the richly painted walls. Scenes from the life of Christ, the stations of the cross, ancient monks and holy men stared back at them.

Harald, having been inside the cathedral on only one occasion before, stood in silent prayer for a few moments, remembering his friends and shipmates on the voyage to the new lands and the loss of Jamie Gunn. Sighing, he returned his thoughts to the present and offered prayers for his two grandsons and their families. He felt a hand on his sleeve and looked down to find Haakon and Jon had come close to his side. He smiled at them and pointed to a large stone pillar nearby.

"Therein lie the cleft skull and bones of St. Magnus," he told them. Both boys drew in a sharp breath.

"How did they get into the pillar?" whispered Jon, sensing some magic at hand.

"He was murdered," Harald explained, "and laid to rest at Birsay. People came to pay their respects and were cured of their ills, so his nephew, Earl Rognavald Kolson, built this cathedral and laid his uncle's poor bones to rest in that pillar."

Eventually Harald led the boys out of the shadowed cavern of the cathedral and into the blazing afternoon sun. Finding a well, they sipped the cool, sparkling water from cupped hands. Harald dampened his face and suggested they should begin to make for home. So, each cherishing his own vivid memories of the day, they walked back in companionable silence.

# TREASURE

**m**athild placed a shawl about her shoulders and strolled out to meet the weary threesome ambling slowly up the dusty track. "You look tired, son. Take your grandfather and Jon up to the house. There's plenty of food for you all."

Taking the reins from Haakon's hand, Mathild led the pony to the earth-house beside the croft to place the stores beneath the drystone chambered passage—a method of storage which had been used by the islanders for hundreds of years. After turning the pony out to grass, Mathild carried salt, some baskets of flax and malt into the house.

Haakon and Jon chattered noisily as they supped the good, hot broth, recalling the sights of the day. The cathedral, the market, soldiers with swords marching towards the castle, ships, shops and alleyways were conjured up in detail inside the little kitchen.

The evening grew cooler and Jon's father arrived to fetch his son, but Haakon, much impressed with what he had seen of Earl Henry's castle, insisted on recounting further details to his audience: the coat-of-arms above the gate, the battlements and turrets. He could readily imagine the soldiers barracked inside the thick stone walls.

"It's high time you were both away to your beds," scolded the boy's grandfather, smiling fondly at them. Mathild agreed and so Uncle Erik took Jon home, leaving a very drowsy but happy Haakon to slip into bed.

"Thank you for taking the boys to Kirkwall," Mathild whispered to her father. "Such a grand outing for them both."

They smiled at each other and then glanced over at the sleeping boy. A halo of blond hair framed his angular face, its fair, freckled skin browned by the sun. The sea-blue eyes were now closed to the sights of the day, but open to the visions of dreams.

"He is longing to hear of your voyage with Earl Henry, father."

"Many people are full of questions about the voyage, my dear. When we are gathered on the solstice at the Earl's table, the story will be told."

"Is there some secrecy surrounding the voyage?" Mathild persisted.

"Aye, daughter, Earl Henry has many enemies in the English camp, all greedy to get their hands on information. These men are willing to kill the Earl and the Templar Knights; you know how long they have been persecuted for their beliefs."

"I know so little about these men," sighed Mathild.

"The Templar Knights were the guardians of the great Temple of Solomon. They had fought in the Crusades and were established to defend the Holy Land and to protect pilgrims who were travelling to Jerusalem, which was thought at that time to be the very center of the world. They learned a great deal from the Arabs in the east: philosophy, science and many secret techniques used in the building of great temples and cathedrals. They also became fabulously wealthy and acquired much land in France, Spain, England and Scotland. All the sea and land trade routes were guarded by these Templars. They became so wealthy that kings and even countries borrowed money from them."

Mathild listened closely in silence.

"The mystery and secrecy surrounding their organisation eventually led to misunderstandings and persecution. Many Templar Knights were

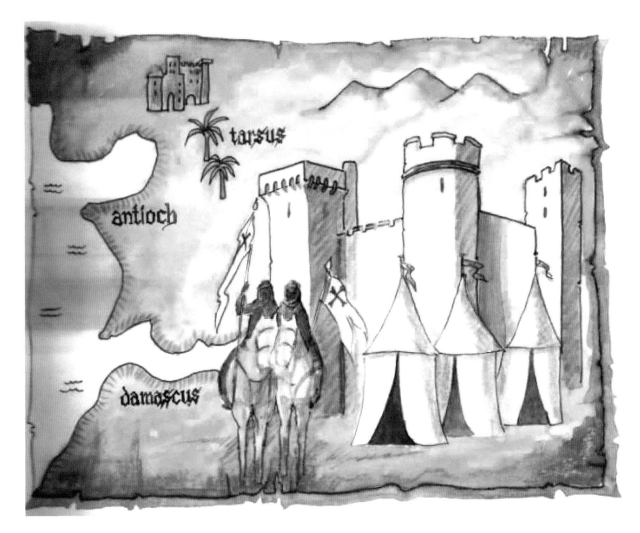

tortured and killed, while others escaped with their wealth. They fled in ships to Portugal and Scotland where the Kings offered them protection.

"The Scottish King, Robert the Bruce, was aided by Knights Templars in his victory at the Battle of Bannockburn in 1314. The St. Clair family has always fought alongside the Templars who settled near Rosslyn Castle. Indeed, our own Earl was born and reared in these Templar traditions at Rosslyn."

"So Sir Henry could be killed through fear, father, and we would lose our good Earl?"

"The man is always at risk, Mathild. He has killed many men over the years to protect his family and lands.  He's  a fine swordsman and always

uses his skill to see that justice is done. The English are a warmongering nation and would love to overthrow our Earl, but fear not, daughter, the fortress at Kirkwall is strong enough to resist those who wish to destroy the man."

Feeling comforted by these words, Mathild stacked more peat upon the fire and, after bidding her father goodnight, she made ready for bed.

The old man sat for awhile in the still house, knowing deep in his heart the full danger that surrounded Earl Henry St. Clair.

A fortnight before midsummer, when the islands were basking in the

warm sun, the homesteaders made good use of the fine weather to repair their crofthouses and barns. Barley and oats ripened in the heat as mild breezes whispered over the fertile fields.

The humble stone-walled dwellings took a continuous battering from strong winds most of the year round. The roofs of thatch and turf, lashed with binders and weighed with heavy boulders, felt keenly the sharp sting of the winter gales. Now, the men cut new turf and repaired walls and thatches while women and children gathered seaweed along the shore to spread out on the land.

As her father, helped by Haakon, strengthened their old crofthouse against the onslaught of the coming winter, Mathild prepared a brew of ale for the midsummer festival. A neighbor, newly returned from Kirkwall, stopped to pass a moment with Harald, saying he had heard that the Earl had returned from Rosslyn yesterday with a company of friends and family — guests for the feast day.

A skirmish had apparently taken place whilst the Earl's ship was at sea. A band of ruffians out for blood and loot had foolishly attacked Henry's ship, only to be set upon by soldiers and knights of the House of St. Clair. Minor injuries had been sustained by Henry's men, but the brigands had come off worse and finally limped away to the mainland to nurse their wounds.

Haakon and his grandfather listened and smiled, imagining the scene. Unknown vessels were frequently spotted around the islands which were now under the Earl's protection from pirates and smugglers. Merchant ships needing a safe harbour to unload their cargo of flax, timber, pitch and salt were regularly piloted into the Bay of Kirkwall. They collected fish, pork, sheep and hides produced by the islanders who were now prospering under Henry's rule.

Earl Henry had helped to recover land stolen many years earlier by William, Bishop of Orkney. The people had hated the bishop. Selfish and greedy, he had gleaned his wealth selling land belonging rightfully to them and their families. He had plotted and schemed relentlessly to steal both property and possessions, so a strong hatred for him had grown in the hearts of the people. Henry, also disliking the man, had foreseen a time of reckoning at hand. Then, in 1382, the violence had indeed broken out, and Bishop William was slain. Henry, accompanied by the islanders, had set about looking for ancient boundries and stone markers. Over rough, dark moorland and through wet peat bogs they tramped until the former boundries were recovered. Thus, all lands and properties were returned to the rightful owners and peace reigned under Henry's fair and generous guidance.

A buzz of activity ran through the old crofters' settlement. Mothers busy with baking and brewing for the feast-day shooed their excited children outside to play. Haakon, Jon and Eugenie were given sole charge of several small brothers and sisters, a basket of food, and instructions to take them to the beach but to keep them away from the perilous cliffs and return them home before the tide turned.

"Let's look for treasure down at the cove," begged a small voice.

"All right," agreed the two older boys after some discussion. Haakon and Jon marched forwards, remembering the soldiers at Kirkwall, and the straggle of followers skipped along behind with Eugenie carrying the food basket at the rear.

Looking for treasure was a game the children loved. Wrecks were common in these waters and ships, caught unawares by gales and pounding seas, regularly spilled wreckage and cargo along the ragged shoreline. Many a family spent time retrieving this valuable debris from the clutches of the sea. It was treasure indeed!

Sea birds wheeled overhead as the ragtag army reached the shore and Eugenie set the basket down. The tide was out, exposing a vast stretch of sandy beach. Rock pools invited the children to share their secrets. Small

fingers poked at the peaceful anemones asleep in the warm shallows and sent tiny crabs scuttling for shelter under the weeds.

Wandering unhurriedly along the line of flotsam, the children collected their treasures from amongst the broken masts, torn canvas and scraps of frayed rope bleached white by the sun.

Eugenie, walking with Bella, noticed her small cousin pick up something shiny.

"May I see what you've found, Bella?" she inquired."

"No, it's my special treasure." Bella insisted, not wanting to reveal her find.

"I won't tell, I promise," Eugenie persisted.

Reluctantly, Bella handed over a large, silver brooch to her cousin.

"Oh, it's lovely!" sighed Eugenie.

"What's lovely?" asked Jon, who, on seeing the glint of silver had wandered with eager curiosity towards the two girls.

"Please don't let him have it!" cried Bella.

Drawn to the small girl's urgent cries, Haakon and the others hurried to the spot. Bella protested still louder as they all examined the brooch.

"Hey, that's just like the pin I saw on Earl Henry's cloak!" Haakon exclaimed. "Perhaps he lost it when he last sailed to Scotland. Best take care of it. Grandfather can give it back to him at the feast."

"But it's mine, I found it!" exclaimed Bella indignantly. She was now in tears, remembering her mother's words: 'The leavings of the sea belong to whoever finds them.'

"You would be thrown into the dungeons at Kirkwall and never seen again if Earl Henry found out that you had stolen it," whispered one of the younger boys.

"Leave her be, she hasn't stolen anything," broke in Eugenie, coming to Bella's defence. "I'm sure Earl Henry would never throw any of his people into dungeons. He's a kind man. He might even reward Bella for finding his pin."

Placing her arm protectively around the still-sobbing Bella, Eugenie led the children away from the driftwood and back to the basket of food. They sat on the warm sand and ate their fill in thoughtful silence. When the food was all gone, Eugenie wrapped up the silver brooch in a frayed linen napkin and placed it carefully at the bottom of the basket with a flat stone on top.

"Let's look for more treasure," cried Jon eagerly. Then, jumping to his feet, he set off once again towards the tideline. The boys now spread out in earnest across the beach. Eugenie and Bella, however, were content to lie on the warm sand, playing with the pretty shells and coloured glass until, feeling drowsy from the sun, both girls fell fast asleep.

Screaming gulls and a shouting voice woke Eugenie from her dreams. Haakon was running towards her.

"Have you seen William?" he called breathlessly.

"We've been asleep," Eugenie replied and sat up, rubbing her eyes. "I haven't seen William at all. I thought he went with you. It's late," she went on, sensing now that something was wrong, "We must get back soon."

"We've got to find William first. He's wandered off somewhere." Haakon looked anxiously up and down the beach. Eugenie got to her feet.

"Call Jon and the others; we'll all search together."

"Jon is already searching at the far end of the cove." Haakon pointed away towards the distant headland. "Come with me, Eugenie. Bella, you stay here with the basket. We'll soon return with William," Haakon added, not wanting to alarm the small girl any more than he had already done.

"You will be quite safe here. Just stay close to the path," Eugenie encouraged her. She gave the small child a kiss and told her how important it was to look after the basket with its secret treasure.

Feeling assured now that her cousins would not be away too long, Bella agreed and smiled at them weakly, holding her wooden doll and basket close to her body.

The two older children at once turned and followed the long line of debris left by the tide, noticing with relief a set of small footprints in the wet sand.

"Hurry!" called Haakon, running on ahead until the footprints stopped in front of an outcrop of rocks.

"Can you climb?" he asked Eugenie as she caught up with him. "William must have gotten over somehow."

They scrambled up the steep rocks, sharp barnacles scraping their bare feet. The tide was coming in. A dozen gulls and skewers argued and squawked over a dead fish. Shading their eyes, they saw only more beach, of shingle and patchy sand now, more rocks and a distant cave.

"That's it!" exclaimed Haakon. "A cave, and look—more footprints!"

Racing along the shingle, they soon came to an enormous, gaping hollow in the cliff face. Moving eagerly forwards, they discovered with disappointment that its dark interior stopped short at a wall of solid rock. Not yet ready to give up, they explored the wet surface carefully.

"Look, here's another footprint!" called Eugenie excitedly from behind a rock close to the cliff face. Haakon joined her. She had discovered an angled fissure large enough for the children to squeeze through. It opened out into a shadowy passageway. Water dripping from the roof made the walls shiny and the floor beneath their feet changed from cold wet sand to hard dry rock, and seemed to them to ascend.

"Are you alright?" Haakon whispered. Eugenie reached out for his hand.

"I think so. Please, let's go on."

Squinting in the darkness, Haakon and Eugenie felt their way along the passage by touching the walls of the cave. A pale glow some way ahead gradually grew brighter, revealing a larger opening turning away to the left. Hardly daring to breathe, they crept forwards.

Bella, waiting back at the cove, caught sight of Jon and the others making their way from the headland. Jumping up, she waved her shawl excitedly, calling them to hurry. The boys ran swiftly towards the frantic child, surprised to find that Haakon and Eugenie had deserted her.

"They've been g-g-gone for ages and the tide is c-c-coming in." she stammered tearfully, still clutching the basket. "Please run home and fetch Grandfather. We must find all the others before it gets dark."

"I'll go," said Jon. "Keep Bella with you and make your way home."

They watched him sprint across the beach and up over the heather towards the village.

"Listen!" whispered Eugenie, squeezing Haakon's hand to emphasise her command. A barely audible sound reached their ears from up ahead.

"It could be the tide coming in," said Haakon anxiously, sensing that the sea would now be drawing somewhere near the cave entrance.

"No, listen again." A faint ripple of sound echoed through the passageway.

"It's a cry. Someone's crying and calling. It's William, I'm sure!"

Pulling at his hand, she plunged headlong through the darkness. A dank, musty smell mingling with the chill of the air made her shiver. Fascination and fear gripped them both.

The passage ended abruptly and a steep slope of rock plunged away before them into a gigantic cavern. Rays of light filtered through narrow slits somewhere high up in the roof. The astonished children gazed about in wonder. As their eyes grew more accustomed to the dim light, they took in the scene before them. The small boy was sitting forlornly some distance away, surrounded by oak coffers and wooden chests. Ropes, oars and broken lanterns lay strewn across the rocky floor as if the owners had left in some haste.

"William!" Eugenie called softly, not wanting to alarm him.

"Hullo!" boomed a man's voice from out of the darkness.

"Who was that?" Unnerved by the unexpected voice, Eugenie clung to Haakon's arm as they slithered down the rocky slope of the cave floor. Sobbing with relief, William ran into the arms of his two cousins, and their warm embraces soon restored his natural confidence.

"Look what I've found. Real treasure! And it's all mine!" He beamed up at them.

Again the man's voice boomed. It was closer this time. Haakon carefully drew William and Eugenie into the shadows, silencing them with a stern look. The three anxious children watched as men emerged from a dark tunnel at the far end of the cavern. But their fear turned to relief and delight as they recognised their grandfather leading the way, followed by Jon's father, Erik. Next came soldiers armed with longswords and then Earl Henry himself. The children left their hiding place and ran eagerly towards their rescuers.

"Thank God you're safe," rejoiced the old man.

"Jon found a very worried Bella waiting for you on the beach. He ran all the way home and told us you were missing," Uncle Erik explained.

Earl Henry took up the story. "I was visiting your grandfather when the boy, Jon, came with the news. Fortunately, Harald remembered these old caves and so we have a boat alongside to take you home." He hesitated as his gaze was caught by the wooden chests. "What have we here?"

"Looks like the spoils of pirates and smugglers, my Lord," put in Erik. He raised his lantern to make a closer inspection easier. Henry lifted the lid of the coffer. Silver plates, goblets and coins of gold glinted in the soft glow. Another chest revealed more silver, wax candles and an aged hourglass. Manuscripts decorated with gilded scenes of birds and animals, maps and scrolls of yellowed parchment tied about with faded silk ribbons—all lay patiently awaiting their discovery. Flagons of red wine lay stacked against the wooden chests.

"Put the coffers into the boat, we will leave the rest. I want to get these children safely home to their families," Earl Henry instructed his men.

Leading the way, the men carried the heavy contraband through the dark tunnel. Eugenie and Haakon followed, tightly gripping William's hands between them. At the cave entrance, the sun dazzled their eyes. The low tide, now at its height, lapped the wide ledge of rock on which they stood. A longboat, held off the rocks by a steady and experienced hand, was soon maneuvered into a good position to take the party of children on board. Placing the coffers at the bottom of the boat, the men took up their positions then rowed away from the cliffs and out into the open sea.

A crowd of onlookers who had gathered up on the cliff top now cheered heartily as the longboat came into sight. Harold signalled that the children were safe and the people ran down towards the beach as the rowers pulled around the dangerous rocks and into the narrow cove. Gratefully, Haakon spotted his mother amongst the crowd. Eugenie's mother was there too, wiping tears from her eyes, and William's mother ran into the sea, oblivious to the cold, as the boat was hauled onto the shingle. A mixture of both anger and joy was clear in her voice as she scolded her small son.

**The Earl stood up and helped the children to the shore.**

"Be proud of your children — they have shown great courage!" he told the women and winked at Haakon. Then turning to Harald he said, "Bring the children to Kirkwall for the feast and they shall be well rewarded for this day's adventure."

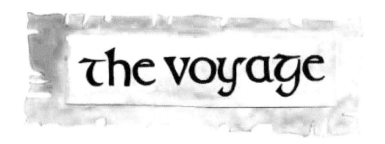

# the voyage

**B**right beacon fires could be seen across the high points of the islands. The midsummer celebrations had begun. Kirkwall bustled with activity and Haakon, Mathild and Harald strolled amongst the crowds, looking at the stalls in the marketplace.

Noticing his daughter's expressive face as she gazed longingly at some bales of blue silk, Harald led the two away from the market and down through a narrow street towards the castle.

"You look fine, my dear, in your homespun gown with your golden hair about your shoulders," he told his daughter.

Mathild smiled gracefully at her father, throwing her shawl over her arm. Along the road they joined other families, and eager children ran ahead as the merry procession made its way to the castle.

Haakon gazed in wonder at the high walls. The St. Clair coat-of-arms with its engrailed cross upon the shield stood high above his head as they passed through the huge, stone gateway. All those men who had sailed with Sir Henry were now entering the castle with their wives and children as guests of the Earl and his Lady.

The courtyard was full of noblemen, knights and gentlefolk. The Lady Janette, surrounded by her children and ladies-in-waiting, chatted readily to many of the guests. The air was alive with excitement.

"Welcome, good people!" Earl Henry cried and raised his arm to silence the crowd. "Come! Let us begin the Solstice Feast."

Following the Earl and his Lady, the guests filed through a high arched doorway into the Great Hall. Sunlight streamed in from tall windows, illuminating the ornate wall tapestries richly embroidered with animals and hunting scenes. Harold pointed to the Sword of Sigurd which hung, as he had described, above the wide fireplace, its long, scarred blade glinting in the firelight. Proudly, he led his daughter and grandson to one of the three large wooden tables already lavishly set for feasting. Each person stood respectfully as Earl Henry and Lady Janette took their place of honour. Henry then motioned to all present to be seated, and steaming food was brought on trenchers to the three tables. The bustle of servants and the enjoyment of the guests made the event so exciting that Haakon could hardly eat! He glanced across to where Jon and Eugenie sat, catching their eyes. All three grinned at each other conspiratorially. The wine flowed and glasses were raised in celebration as still more food was served.

The guests were now at ease, their hunger and thirst sated. A Templar knight in his white robes stood up to raise his goblet of wine.

"Let us all stand and raise our glasses to our noble brother, Sir Henry St. Clair, Earl of Orkney, Baron of Rosslyn, Premier Earl of Norway — a brave and gallant man. May your life be long, Sir Henry, with your beloved family and devoted subjects of Orkney."

Everyone raised their glasses and cheered, and the Templar knight sat down again. Then another man stood up to honour his Earl — Sir Antonio Zeno, tall and imposing. He waited patiently for the cheering to subside, then began his speech.

"I also wish to honour our most generous Prince Zichmi," he told the assembled party. Once more, glasses were raised.

"Who is Prince Zichmi?" whispered Haakon into his grandfather's ear. Harald answered in a low voice.

"'Tis a name Sir Antonio has given to Henry. He has trouble saying 'St. Clair' because his language is different from ours. Sometimes he calls Henry 'Principe Enrico', but we all know who he means. Antonio sees Earl Henry as a prince because of his position as Earl of Orkney and Premier Earl of Norway."

Haakon was satisfied and impressed with his answer. If Earl Henry was a prince then he was royal indeed! Haakon felt very important to be present at the feast in the castle.

Sir Antonio remained standing and continued, telling the gathering how he had written an account of the life of the Prince, sending many letters to his brother, Carlo, in Venice. He described how he had brought maps and sea-charts from his country, and a compass and navigational techniques which had proved invaluable to Henry. With the additional charts and maps belonging to the Knights Templar, a plan was drawn up to raise a fleet of ships and open a new trade route across the Atlantic to the islands in the west. The Templars wished to find new lands to colonise, and this could prove to be a prosperous trade link, giving Earl Henry the sea-power he needed.

"We heard of a paradise across the ocean, a fertile land with good timber forests and rivers brimming with fish and cities of gold, ruled by kings adorned with gold and bright feathers. An old fisherman who had come to this place by chance told us his story and agreed to be our guide."

Haakon remembered his grandfather's story of the fisherman.

"Our preparations were made."

The Great Hall became hushed and still. Those who had taken part in the voyage prepared to relive it, while those who had not yet been told

**Coat-of-Arms of Jarl Henry St. Clair**

the details listened closely. This was the story they had been waiting for. Antonio continued to speak.

"We had our compass, sand-glass and sea-charts. We provisioned our fleet of twelve ships, fully crewed with two hundred Templar men-at-arms, stores of food and dried fish, seeds and grain, animals and farm implements. We took medicines for our bodies, a priest for our souls and forge for our cannon and armour."

Here Antonio paused to nod in the direction of Harald, who bowed, acknowledging the generous recognition.

"Sir James Gunn, our brother Templars, a party of Cistercian monks and many of the craftsmen you see here among us today, made up our number." Again Antonio paused to acknowledge the carpenters, sailmakers, masons and shipbuilders and their families seated at the tables before continuing. "I was not the chief command," he smiled, "as Prince Zichmni himself came as our Lord, and I was appointed Admiral. Luck was not on our side, for three days before our departure, the old fisherman died. We could not give up, however, and so persuaded some of the sailors who had been with the man originally to accompany us. We then set sail on the first day of April, 1398, from Bress in Shetland. The wind was in our favour, and soon we came to the Faroe Islands where we took on fresh water and supplies. Afterwards, we made straight for the open sea, but it was not long before there arose a great storm. For eight days we were tossed and driven we know not where, but at length the storm abated. We gathered together our scattered vessels and sailed on for ten days west and south-west in the rough seas with a following wind."

At this point, Earl Henry stood up, indicating that he wished to speak.

"I have never sailed with men so brave. We experienced great terror and exhaustion. I am honoured to have known a crew of such gallantry."

Harald and the rest of the crew now openly discussed the hardships of their voyage, vividly recalling the crashing seas and savage gales that had broken a mast in two and strewn cannon across the deck. They remembered the wonder of sighting whales on the journey, their huge tails thrashing the foaming water before silently vanishing into its cold depths. Giant icebergs had drifted past their tiny ships and fear had torn into the men's hearts as the vast sea enveloped them, seeming to swallow their very souls. Exhausted himself, Earl Henry had yet given new courage to his men, urging them onwards on the darkest of nights when many a brave man would have turned back. Salt winds had cut into their blistered faces as they sailed on into the blackness. They had thought of the old sea gods and shivered as hunger and thirst gnawed at their frail bodies.

Again the Great Hall grew quiet as the men were silenced by the painful memories of their enormous hardship. Now Sir Antonio took up the story once more.

"We were exhausted and in dire need of fresh water when land was sighted by our crew in the first ship. We did not know what country this was and we were cautious about approaching at first. We saw islands and trees and the weather was fair for, by God's blessing, the wind had lulled and there came a great calm. Some of the crew pulled ashore, later returning to tell us of a safe harbour and an excellent country with fresh water, where game and wildlife were abundant. On their return we refreshed ourselves, for the men had found many sea birds' eggs to stave off our hunger."

Here the men laughed, grimly remembering how sick they had been after eating so many eggs.

"Our priest said prayers for our safe landfall and we finally made the mainland on the 2nd of June, 1398, Trinity Sunday. Looking across this new land we saw in the distance a great hill that poured forth smoke and although it was a long way off, the Prince sent a hundred men to go and explore the country, charging them to bring back an account of the island and its inhabitants. After eight days the soldiers returned, bringing word that they had been across the island and up the smoking hill. The smoke, they discovered, was a natural phenomenon. It proceeded from a great fire in the bottom of the hill, where a certain substance like pitch ran into the sea. They had seen many people, half wild, small in stature and very timid, living in caves thereabouts. They also reported a large river and a good, safe harbour nearby."

Sir Antonio paused to take a drink and Earl Henry rose to his feet. "I could see it was a good country," he told his eager audience, "green and fertile. Indeed it was all that we had heard it to be from our forebears who had reached these shores many years before—men such as Lief Ericsson and Thorfinn Karlsefni. We hoped to find their settlements and I, too, was eager to found a city in this fair land. But I could see so clearly that some of my men were fatigued and so I decided to send them home, before the good weather failed and the onset of winter began. I kept with me our armourer, Harald Haraldsson, sailmakers, masons, and a number of shipbuilders. The Cistercian fathers remained with us, as did our companions and brother knights. I commanded my brave Admiral Antonio to guide my men home, much against his will, with most of our ships, leaving me with small boats and oars."

Antonio now broke in. "I wished truly to stay with our prince on this new land, but as he commanded, I departed sadly with the ships and men. I sailed for twenty days to the east without a glimpse of any land. Then, turning my course towards the south-east, in five days I sighted land and found myself on the island of Neome. Knowing this country, I already perceived I was past Iceland, and as the inhabitants are subject to Prince Zichmni, I took in fresh water and stores and then sailed for three days further to Orcadie, where we were received with a hearty welcome." Having reached the end of his part of the adventure, Sir Antonio bowed and took his seat.

Earl Henry thanked him and then turned towards his wife, friends and subjects, encouraging them to eat and drink their fill upon this good feast day. He then took up his story of the voyage.

"After Antonio and the others had departed we made camp along the shore close to a spring of fresh water and took stock of our stores for the coming winter. As fresh food and water were plentiful upon this land, we planned to provision our small boats and set about to explore our surroundings. After naming our landing Cape Trin we rowed further up the coast to a safe harbour, which we named Trin Harbour. At this time we were watched closely by groups of shy natives, curious at our appearance. Not wishing them to find us enemies, I sent a priest to offer them our friendship. They approached us cautiously and we made signs to each other, for we had no common tongue. A bond was struck between us, however, and I called them 'Mic Mac', which as you know in Gaelic means, 'my beloved sons'. They lived by hunting and fishing, but not by cultivating corn. Dressing only in small breechcloths of animal skin, with cloaks of fur and moccasins of moose hide, these people greased their bodies against the many flies in the summer heat. They wore no headdress and their hair was black or reddish. At their invitation we inspected their weapons; strong bows, stone arrows, and wooden clubs. They speared the fish in the rivers and searched for clams along the shore. Eventually, we taught them how to make nets to fish with and how to cure the meat they hunted.

"Never before having seen iron or money or my 'sword of sharpness', as they called it, they surely believed that I worked magic, thinking that I was a great leader, and they gave me the name 'Glooscap', meaning 'the deceiver of enemies'."

The crowd gathered in the Great Hall cheered and smiled their approval. Henry placed both his hands upon the table and looked intently at the faces before him.

"The only enemies of these people were darkness, storm, rain and winds. We taught them many of our ways and customs, as they taught us theirs, including the shapes of the island and its rivers. They told us of a large, wide bay called 'Owokun' meaning 'where the deep sea dashes.'

"We left the Cistercian fathers to clear land and build a settlement where we had made our first landing, while I set out with a group of men to find this bay called 'Owokun'. We passed the smoking mountain and reached another safe harbour at Pictou, where we found a smoking hole with streams of pitch running into the sea.

"Making camp, we refreshed ourselves at this place, setting off the next day in a north-westerly direction along a wide river and then overland, reaching the wide river basin of 'Owokun' as the sun was setting. Here we discovered that the turbulence of the water caused by a rip-tide emptied the basin of water every twelve hours. The tip of the promontory on which we stood commanded a clear view of the entire coast, so it was decided that this should be used for our winter settlement. A sheltered cove having been sought and found to suit all we might need, my men set about collecting timber and stone for our shelter. Pine-tar and fibres for ropes were also in abundance, so with many skilled hands, the shipwrights soon set to work with axes and adzes preparing the timber for our new ship. The masons found an ample supply of building materials to erect a hall and defences for winter. After several weeks, snow began to fall and the ground froze beneath us; the Mic Macs named our settlement 'a wigwam called winter'. On those cold, clear nights we sat around our fires teaching the Mic Macs the names of the constellations, while they told us in return the legends of the wild animals on their island—the bear and the moose, the otter and the beaver.

"Our thoughts often went out to Antonio, hoping he had made a safe landing in our homeland.

"Having wintered in our new settlement, we made plans to take a party of men and soldiers with good provisions southward to where we had been told the climate would be milder. Leaving sufficient numbers of soldiers to protect our shipwrights and carpenters, we made ready in two boats to row down through the wide bay to explore.

"We had heard of a land called Norumbega," Henry continued eagerly, "peopled with inhabitants from Norway many years before. Vinlandia, too, was marked upon our maps—a paradise filled with lush vines and warm sunshine. We chanced upon many small coves and inlets, all making good harbours, but we saw no people. We brought our boats to safe anchor in the shelter of a beautiful cove, made camp and after food and a sound sleep, planned to explore again this strange land.

"After an hour's march, we saw ahead of us a rise in the land and decided to continue to climb. The steep hill left us breathless and my good friend Jamie Gunn was in much need of rest, suffering from a fierce pain in his chest. Making camp, we saw at once to his comfort, our physician doing all he could to ease the man's distress. But Jamie became worse during the night. Our medicines and prayers sadly had little effect and we watched our loyal companion slip away from us early in the morning.

"Sorrow fell upon us all that day. He had travelled so far with us, and to leave him there upon that lonely hillside was more than we could bear. Unable to carry him with us, we dug a deep hollow and gently layed him to rest, dressed in full armour with his sword at his side. Our good priest offered up prayers as we bowed our heads and bid farewell to our dear friend."

"I then commanded Harald Haraldson to carve upon the gneiss rock-ledge close to the grave the effigy of Sir Jamie Gunn, complete with armour, sword and coat of arms. Our thoughts went to our loved ones across the sea. I longed beyond words to see my dear wife Janette and my beloved children."

The fire in the Great Hall crackled and the assembled group bent their heads as one, in silent memory of Sir James Gunn.

"On the morrow," Henry continued, bringing his guests into the present, "we left the island and set a course which would take us down the coast. Before nightfall, with the wind in our favour, we set up camp for the night. The next day in blazing sunshine, I took a party of men with me to survey what appeared to be a large island. An expanse of level ground lay before us, and beyond that, gentle hills and woods which would supply much timber. I ordered the masons to set to work with plans to build a large round tower. Six ells was the diameter of the base of the tower and each column measured one ell*. Several longhouses were erected to house the builders and their families who found the island pleasant and wished to remain there.

"When the tower was finished and our survey of the island was complete, we gathered one evening to rest and say prayers, giving thanks for the good fortune that had fallen upon us, for this new found land, a paradise indeed; we wished good fortune to the small band of settlers who planned to stay behind and make a new life on these beautiful shores.

"Myself and the rest of my crew returned to base camp, finding work had begun in our absence on a ship large enough to weather the voyage home the following spring. A keel had been laid and work was well underway. Strong sails, made under cover during the long winter months from our supplies of wadmal, now lay ready. The Mic Macs, who watched us closely, were somewhat bewildered at our comings and goings about the islands. They called our longhouse 'an up-turned canoe' and our ship 'a great whale with trees upon its back'. They prepared furs and pelts, bound with strips of hide, for our return journey, along with maize, a quantity of grapes, dried meat and fresh water.

*an ell was an old Germanic measurement equivalent to a cubit, measured by the length of a man's arm from his elbow to the tip of his middle finger.

That night we feasted and told our guests, the Mic Mac people, that I would return as their friend, not to rule over them or take them as slaves, for they were a gentle people who had shown us nothing but kindness during our stay on their island.

A tremendous sadness was felt by both the crew and the Mic Macs as we hauled the new ship down the beach into the water. With so much to do before the tide turned, we bade them our final farewells and prepared our sails as a good breeze took us gently out into the open bay. We waved back at the cheering crowd of Mic Macs and headed out for deeper water. Sailing for several miles, we eventually reached the original landfall and met with the Cistercian fathers once more. We told them of our achievements and of the islands to the south, as they spoke of their wish to remain on their newly cultivated land, having now produced their first crops.

Earl Henry paused and smiled as he surveyed the assembled guests.

"I shall soon bring my story to a close, good subjects. Thank you for your patience. After bidding farewell to the Fathers, we set our sails with the Gulf Stream and headed south-east towards home, looking back one last time to the coast where our companion, Jamie Gunn, lay buried. The winds were fair and we made good headway, sea birds following us for part of the way. At night the skies were so clear that the stars appeared to be within our grasp. Then, being calm for several days with just a light breeze within our sails, we were able to take rest with only one man at the watch. Once some distance from the land, we came upon a dead whale, its skin covered in weed and crustacean. Some of our men jumped onto its back with great excitement, but the poor whale was merely sleeping, wearied by his long journey. Slowly he began to move, rising his high tail before diving into the cold, dark water. We barely had enough time to pull our men back on board ship. I can assure you, much laughter rang out across our vessel for the rest of that day!"

The company in the Great Hall laughed too.

"And the rest you know," concluded Earl Henry, "for we sailed with a fair wind behind us all the way across the great ocean and home to Orkney."

Enthralled by the account of the long voyage, the guests exchanged animated conversation. Silencing the crowd, a Templar knight, with longsword at his side, stood up next to Henry and, placing an arm around his brother knight, he addressed the gathered throng.

"We shall build new ships and return to Estoiland to found a great city, and we shall invite you in good faith, to bring your families and livestock and sail with us to that fertile and prosperous land."

Loud applause and cheering filled that Great Hall. Glasses were raised once again in honour of the Earl and all the men and women who had sailed with him on his successful voyage to the New World.

# the burial

It was now late. The midnight sun lay just above the horizon as candles were lit in the Hall. The feasting continued throughout the night as many tired children slept while their fathers recalled the old stories and legends of their island home. Lively music sweetened the air, inviting the company of lords and ladies to dance in a swirl of colour.

Across the islands torches were lit from the midsummer fires and taken aloft through farms and fields to ward off evil and prevent the blighting of crops. Young men leaped through the solstice flames as their forefathers had done before them, ensuring fertility for the coming year. The island folk would talk of this feast-day for many months.

*****

As he strolled beside his mother and grandfather across the heather on the return home, Haakon did nothing but dream of a chance to sail with Earl Henry on his next voyage. Haakon and Mathild asked innumerable questions and Haakon was happy to tell them of the new land and described all that they had found there.

A week passed. Antonio Zeno now wished to be away from Orkney, to return to his native Venice and join his brother Carlo and their family. In preparation for the leave-taking he invited Earl Henry to ride out across the island with him to call on several of his loyal crew to bid them farewell. Harald was the first to receive the two men, asking them into the small crofthouse with a warm welcome. Earl Henry asked if the children could be present and so Mathild called to Haakon who was in the barn and he ran to fetch Jon and Eugenie.

The three children arrived and stood in silence while Earl Henry went out to his horse, returning in a few moments with a leather saddlebag. He placed the bag upon the floor and then, from under his cloak, he produced a beautifully engraved longsword. Everyone in the room held their breath as the Earl presented the sword to Haakon.

"This is for you, young man, for the courage you showed in rescuing young William and uncovering the treasure in the cave."

Wide-eyed at the unexpected gift, Haakon managed a whispered "Thank you." Then finding his voice at last, he thanked the Earl a little louder and bowed gracefully.

"It will serve you well when you are full-grown and sail upon the sea as your grandfather has done," said Henry.

Taking in a deep breath, Eugenie then stepped forward nervously and handed to Earl Henry the brooch she had been keeping.

"Haakon thought this was yours, Sir. Bella found it on the beach the day we left for the cave; she gave it to me in return for my best woolen shawl."

Henry drew back his cloak to reveal his own silver pin.

"I have mine, as you can see, but it was honest of you to keep it for me. Now it shall really be yours," and he handed the brooch back to Eugenie, "to wear on a fine gown, young lady," he added, smiling at the blushing girl.

"And you, young sir," he looked at Jon, "Are you to be a shipbuilder like your father?"

"Oh yes, Sir, I am to become an apprentice to my father, Sir."

Smiling at the lad, Earl Henry opened the leather saddle-bag and took from it a small ship modelled on the Venetian galley of Antonio Zeno, complete with tiny cannon.

"Perhaps you will build ships such as this?" Antonio smiled, taking the model from Earl Henry and offering it to Jon. Overwhelmed by their generosity, Jon thanked the Venetian and bowed to the Earl.

The children left the men to talk, and ran out into the sunshine to examine their new treasures.

When Earl Henry and Antonio Zeno came out of the croft, the children ran back to stand before Harald and Mathild, waving their goodbyes as the two men rode away over the moor.

Haakon and his grandfather spent that evening together examining the sword, turning it this way and that in the glowing twilight. Mathild felt proud of her son. She had asked her father to teach the boy his skills as a blacksmith, to give him some expertise other than farming and fishing. She knew Haakon would learn well and that he could become as efficient as her father, and so well able to serve the island folk.

The month of August arrived. The farmers prepared for the harvest and Earl Henry caught up with his manifold duties. One night, a fleet of ships crept under the cover of darkness into the wide bay of Scapa Flow. It was the English who had come to invade the islands of Orkney. As Earl Henry was not at Rosslyn at this time to defend the southern road from London, King Henry the Fourth of England had been confident enough to invade Scotland, and had reached Edinburgh. Sir Robert Logan, the Scottish commander, had been taken captive and thus the way was clear for the attacking English to sail at night across the Pentland Firth to Orkney to challenge Sir Henry St. Clair. With only a mile and a half to Kirkwall, the soldiers armed themselves and prepared to march.

One of Earl Henry's watchmen, positioned on a high point, had seen the ships approaching and hurriedly sent word to the castle. Awakened with the news, the Earl was furious at the eminent invasion and shouted for horses, armour and weapons to repel the invaders before they could burn and spoil the farms and homelands. He was counseled to remain within the keep and to barricade the castle against attack, but that was not the way of a St. Clair. Henry thought only of his subjects, now suffering at the hands of the English.

So it was that Earl Henry St. Clair and his men galloped out into the night to meet their enemy. Close to Scapa Flow they encountered a large armed force of English soldiers. Far outnumbered, Henry and his men fought bravely, helped by the homesteaders in a desperate attempt to protect their lands.

Before long, Harald awoke hearing the shouts and cries and realised that there was trouble on the island. Dressing quickly, he seized his sword and ran to join the group of men making for the high hills above the village. Great fires could be seen, the tall flames licking the night sky. Burning crofts seemed to illuminate the whole island as the now-retreating English made for their ships, at last outnumbered in their turn by men and soldiers returning from Kirkwall.

Haakon hurriedly pulled on his clothes and ran to call Jon who was already on his way over. They followed their grandfather and watched, elated, as the enemy ships sailed out into the protection of the open sea.

"We've beaten them!" cried the boys.

"English dogs!" shouted a man close by.

"Cowards and heathens!" added another.

A horse and rider raced wildly up the hill towards the indignant crowd.

"They've got our Jarl!" he shrieked.

There was confusion at the news. "What, captured the man?"

"No! Done for him! Cruelly slain he is, and bleeding in the heather!" replied the breathless rider.

A cry of pain went up as the crowd of men poured down over the hillside towards their dying Earl. Word had been sent to Lady Janette at the castle. The grief-stricken islanders followed the party of soldiers and loyal knights as they gently carried Henry's broken body back to Kirkwall. The people of Orkney were dazed by the tragedy. Haakon and his family mourned the loss of the gentle man who had visited them only the week before. Antonio Zeno, although ready to return to Venice, was requested to remain on the island to guide and serve the Earl's son and heir, for, not being a sea-going man, he needed the expertise of his father's Admiral.

Sir Antonio, the prospects of returning soon to his homeland now dashed, wrote once more to his brother—his last letter home.

Before long, the news had reached Orkney that the people of Rosslyn had witnessed a 'great light about the castle', as if 'all were on fire', on the very night Henry had been slain, fulfilling the ancient legend that surrounded the death of the Lairds of St. Clair, that the castle at Rosslyn would seem to glow with light as if it were burning and on fire.

The body of Earl Henry was carefully anointed and dressed in armour. Then, accompanied by his brothers, the Templar Knights, Henry was placed upon a bier and taken to his longship, which bore the engrailed

Dear Carlo

Concerning those things that you desire to know of me as to the people & their habits, the animals & countries adjoining, I have written about them in a separate book which please God, I shall bring with me when I return home. In it I have described the country, the customs and laws of Frisland, Island, Estland, Orchadie, the kingdom of Norway, Estotiland & Drogio. I have also described the exploration of Engroneland by our brother, Nicolo, & the settlement that he founded. I will say no more of this in my letter, but hope to be with you very shortly to satisfy your curiosity on these & other subjects by word of mouth. Lastly, I have written of the life & exploits of Zichmni, a prince as worthy of immortal memory as any that lived, for his great bravery and remarkable goodness. —Antonio.

cross on her sail. The Lady Janette, her family and many friends and subjects sailed with the ship carrying the body of Henry out of the bay, across the Pentland Firth, to the mainland and the castle home of the St. Clairs of Rosslyn.

St. Matthew's Church* was filled with drawn, silent faces, many tear-stained, as they paid their last respects to their noble Earl, loving husband and father. A subdued band of men returned miserably to Orkney while Lady Janette, now broken-hearted, remained at Rosslyn with her family.

And so, in the month of August, in the year 1400, and only months after returning from his successful voyage to the New World, Prince Henry St. Clair was laid to rest in full armour without a coffin — an honour usually reserved for royalty, but one which was also granted to the St. Clairs, as guardians of the Holy Rood of Scotland.

**But that is another story.**

*St. Matthews Church refers to the church present before the current Rosslyn Chapel was constructed.

# Epilogue
## For parents and children

There is a growing belief that Prince Henry St. Clair aka Sinclair never returned from his momentous voyage to the New World in 1398, because if he had done so, there would have been a monument erected to him in Orkney or at his family seat at Rosslyn in Scotland where he was born.

It was clear that Henry appreciated the dangers of the voyage, because prior to his departure, he made provision for the division of his property among members of his family. On the other hand, it may have been his intention to remain in the New World to strengthen the growing trading links between Europe and America (as it came to be known). In reality, it was an ambitious plan to create a Norse Northern Commonwealth—a long-time ambition of the Norsemen since the time of King Knut (Canute) of Denmark who conquered England in 1016 and made his capitol in London. By marrying Emma St. Clair, the widow of the disposed King Ethelred 'the Unready', he gained much-needed Norman support because the Sinclairs, although of Viking descent, made their home in Normandy at Castle St. Clair-sur-Epte. The French King, Charles 'the Simple', had assigned the province of Neustria to Hrolf 'the Granger' on condition that he and his Vikings cease raiding the coast of France. So many Norsemen arrived that Neustria soon became known as North-men's Land or Normandy, as it is still known to this day. With the introduction of surnames in the eleventh century, the Sinclair / St. Clair family took their name from St. Clair-sur-Epte.

The Norse Northern Commonwealth which was envisioned would have included:

> The three Scandinavian countries of Norway, Sweden and Denmark which had been united by Queen Margrette of Norway by the Treaty of Kalmar in 1397.

Scotland, because of the close links between that country and Norway.

England, as can be gathered from the correspondence which had taken place between Queen Margarette and Richard II of England.

The Orkney and Shetland Islands, which were already under the jurisdiction of the Norwegian realm.

The Faroes, Iceland and Greenland, which were also under the jurisdiction of Norway.

Helluland (Labrador), Markland (Newfoundland) and Vinland (the eastern coast of North America which Vikings had been visiting since the eleventh century i.e., since the time of King Knut 'the Great'.

Another reason for believing that Prince Henry died in the New World is the fact that his son, Henry II, was never inaugurated as Earl of Orkney. In 1420, his son, Earl William Sinclair, the subsequent builder of the internationally famous Rosslyn Chapel, was installed as the Earl of Orkney as it was safe to assume that his grandfather, Prince Henry, would be dead.

The Venetian, Antonio Zeno, who had accompanied Prince Henry to the New World, described him in a letter to his brother, Carlo, in Venice as follows: *"If there was ever a man who was worthy of immortal memory, it is this man because of his great bravery and goodness."*

Today, there may be no new land to discover, but there are plenty of fresh discoveries to be made on our own planet and in the Universe beyond. Turn over any stone and you may find an insect that has never been recorded, or look into the night sky and you may see a new planet being born. Henry's grave has still to be discovered. Perhaps that can be your discovery. The new advances in the tracing of DNA will help you to establish his identity from his bones or from a strand of hair which may have survived. But above all, discover yourself and the power which lies within you to change the world around you. Be bold. Be resolute. Be imaginative. You, too, can become worthy of *immortal memory*.

**Niven Sinclair**

# About the Author

I have been involved in many of the creative arts, including illustration and calligraphy, for a great number of years, and have taught this to adults and children as well. I have collaborated with other artists on books on the Worlds of Faerie, worked closely with Brian Froud on the 'Lady Cottington' books as a calligrapher, and produced paintings for a number of galleries on the subjects which inspire me: the sea and the landscape of Dartmoor where I lived.

Growing up by the sea, and spending long days sailing with my grandfather in his fishing boat, having the freedom to explore and investigate, with all manner of adventures, developed my imagination.

I was greatly honoured to be included on the St. Clair Project, and to be invited to write, illustrate and design a book about Sir Henry St. Clair, Earl of Orkney. The research was extremely interesting and exciting. I became totally captivated by the story. I feel today's children, even with all the technology they have to hand, still need to hear the amazing stories and legends that surround our islands, especially about the daring courage of those men who took part in the Crusades and who set out to discover new lands across the Atlantic.

At present I am working on a children's novel about the adventures of a little boy who has embarked on a journey with a group of faerie characters in a quest to rescue a magic Book of Wisdom.

I am also continuing my exploration on canvas into the landscape which I find to be so inspiring.

*Hazel Brown*

Printed in Great Britain
by Amazon

82134347R00060